Women and Theatre

Women and Theatre
Calling the Shots

edited by SUSAN TODD

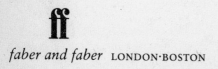

faber and faber LONDON·BOSTON

First published in 1984
by Faber and Faber Limited
3 Queen Square London WC1N 3AU
Printed in Great Britain by
Redwood Burn Limited
Trowbridge Wiltshire

© Liane Aukin, Pam Brighton, Catherine Hayes,
Ann Jellicoe, Meri Jenkins, Bryony Lavery,
Di Seymour, Maggie Steed, Susan Todd,
Harriet Walter, 1984

Library of Congress Cataloging in Publication Data

Main entry under title:

Women and theatre

1. Women in the theater—Great Britain.   I. Todd,
Susan, 1942–
PN2595.W65   1984   792'.088042   83–5571
ISBN 0–571–13042–9 (pbk)

British Library Cataloguing in Publication Data

Women and theatre
1. Women in the theatre—Great Britain
—History—20th Century
I. Todd, Susan
792'.088042   PN2582.W6

ISBN 0–571–13042–9

Contents

Foreword

Most people who do creative work experience at some point the painful inner struggle involved in realizing a project that exists only in the mind. That project can be a book, a play, a painting, a performance. They also experience, if they are fortunate, the transient but joyful feelings of achievement, relief when the work is finished, and the pleasure of sharing it and testing it with others.

Women undergo that struggle to finish the work with particular ferocity. Its forms are in some ways externally determined. It can be hard to gain access to the skills involved, particularly in creative jobs in theatre, say, where an apprenticeship is the best means of learning—in directing, or lighting design, for instance. There is still prejudice against women who want to take a full part in the processes of control and organization through which aesthetic images are made and received.

There are also powerful internal barriers for women in carrying through creative projects. Their historic role as self-abnegating beings, mothering and nurturing others' egos rather than their own, militates against the growth of those more wayward and individualistic desires and the bold imagination required to finish a work of art which can then be shared.

Not all the women who have contributed to this book have experienced their gender as a problem in doing creative work in the theatre. But all have something to say about how they represent their sex and its experiences in their work, and some have something to say about the conflicts they

9

encounter in making their ideas about how to represent women on the stage heard and understood—by themselves as well as for others.

In theatre, pressure comes from the clash and jostle of strong wills meeting together in a complex network of relationships—economic, intellectual, practical consider-ations are all constantly in play. Decisions are swiftly made, and remade, on what for a performer or writer can be crucial points in the interpretation that results in the character image which an audience will see, hear, and carry away as a trace on their consciousness, perhaps for life. Many of the women in this book speak of their hard-won learning, through the experience of work, of how to question and investigate ac-cepted, or masculinist, or fantasized notions of women's be-haviour and perceptions in those small and stressful moments that are fought for before the next shot is called.

SUSAN TODD
March 1983

Right out in front

HARRIET WALTER

When people ask me why I act there's a part of me that says, 'It's simple, it's the same thing that makes a dog want to run very fast.' Now I'm acting every day there's a physical enjoyment that I would miss terribly. I feel for people when they're out of work, not only because there's a lot of self-respect lost, but because that energy has nowhere to go. You can't act alone in your bedroom. You've got to be wanted, and you've got to be put in someone else's play.

When I was nine I was always saying, 'I want to be a film star.' When I'm working in a group, and being all Socialist and thinking 'I'm not in it for my ego' I remember that that core is there: wanting to be watched, wanting to matter, wanting to have everything I think projected on to more people than just those immediately around me.

If there was a moment when I got a shove towards what I do now, it was when I was at boarding school and my parents split up. It was as if there was a direct transfer of energy, from feeling betrayed, that nobody was watching me or loving me, to feeling I'm going to *make* everybody watch me and love me. Every time I walked down the street I imagined there was a film camera on me. (Other actresses have that fantasy too: they make the bed and think there's somebody watching.) The same thing happens when people lose their faith. They can't accept that they're really alone and have to create some kind of substitute for God watching and judging them the whole time. What I'm saying is that for me the acting came from quite an intense source. A fantasy that I was something—and I don't mean just a 'me me me' something

11

but an energy I was aware of, inside, that wasn't about sitting behind a sewing machine or going to school or getting married (which had never interested me anyway). There wasn't a conflict, but rather this energy filling a vacuum.

I found the feeling that I wasn't important very difficult to deal with. At home I was the younger of two daughters and at school I was one of loads of girls. There was a desperation to make my mark—something most other people don't feel so desperate about. You can say either that that's to do with wanting to be creative, or that it's a weakness in people who are creative that they can't accept they're just one of a crowd. I recognize that in myself and it comes back and humbles me at times when I think I'm just getting along being a sensible, mature adult working in a mature world. There is a great need to be special, though it was dormant from when I was about fifteen and showing off at school until a couple of years ago when I started getting a bit of limelight. Before then, it had been 'No, I'm not in it for that, I want to change the world with a group of people.'

I've always taken a pride in doing things well. If I'm being disciplined about making sense of the text, concentrating and allowing things to happen, I feel good in the way you feel good when you get high marks in an exam. Over and above that, very occasionally in performance I've had the sensation of prickles up my spine—like when a really beautiful piece of music takes you by surprise and you go hot and cold and shivery and tears come to your eyes. I've never had an individual high of the 'Oh they're all looking at me isn't it wonderful!' kind. You have to be so self-conscious and self-critical that you can never allow yourself to take off like that. There have been highs to do with an occasion. If the play you're doing—its message, or just the fact that it's happening at all—has meant something tremendous to the group of people you're playing to, that can be a great celebration. Playing *Marat-Sade* in Soweto was like that. In the end it was the event that had taken place that was thrilling, and that event was made up of the fact that we'd come there, that we were defying the authorities, that we sang together at the end. I thought this force could change the world.

When you grow up in acting, you have to come to terms with the fact that your self is very small. It's not true to say actors are egoists. You can become bigger individually as a film star or pop star—or you can do it with a group of people, and together you can create something extraordinary. What moves me, in any art, is the impulse behind it rather than what's said: the fact that somebody needed to write that song, paint that picture, and assumed we would understand.

Your own privacy, feelings and emotions are the source of the communication that you make onstage. But once you go out and do it, you have to put that subjective experience behind you. You delve into what you have felt, have remembered feeling, but then you have to sell it, communicate it. It doesn't matter if you're not feeling it. You've observed that state and you've thought about that person. You've already done the thinking and feeling. Onstage you have to take off on to a different level. Personally, having been quite inhibited and shy, it's a kind of extroversion experience, in which you suddenly find you're not questioning or thinking about yourself and where your hands are. You're right out in front and something else is doing it for you. Sometimes you come offstage and say, 'Someone else was out there tonight—I don't know who was acting it, it wasn't me.'

I very rarely let go, release, and as a feminist I've thought that's to do with my upbringing. It is very hard for women to let go, to show off, to release anger onstage, or cry. I find that very inhibiting, perhaps because of not wanting to play on that side of my nature, so it becomes private and I don't want to have to show it. I'd love to see if I could go crazy—I'd find that hard. I've found though that lots of parts don't demand that release of feeling, and so a lot of my acting is to do with restraint, holding back. I get described as someone who can put over withheld emotion, that range of controlled feeling. Directors always seem to want me to be soft. At a moment

13

when the character might choose either to mask her feelings a little and be a bit witty or to cry, the director will want me to cry. My complaints are minimal compared with friends' experiences of being stereotyped, but there is that pressure to be soft and sensitive and vulnerable, because that's what they've decided I'm good at—just as they've decided that other people are good at being funny, or tough, or witty.

I get fed up that not so much is required of actresses as of actors. Look at the films of *Hamlet* and *Chimes at Midnight*—both have parts in them that I've played. The Lady Percy had long blonde hair, spoke with a lisp, simpered and kissed Hotspur goodbye. All her speeches were cut. The Ophelia was very pretty, obviously burgeoning sexually, and then went a bit loony. That was all that was required of those actresses. An actor, male or female, should have the same skills—of observation, of sustaining a part, of imaginative leaps—just as a carpenter, male or female, must have the same skills. But so many parts for women don't require the exercise of those techniques. Now you have an evolution of male expectations of women and their craft: 'That's all right, that's lovely what you're doing,' and they don't want you to go beyond it. From that point of view women have to be bolder with themselves. If you meet only what is required of you, you have only yourself to blame if you're pigeon-holed. Men quite often grow and their talents leap because the part requires it of them. They either meet the challenge or they don't. I know given the challenge I've always responded. You just hope and pray you'll go on being invited. The men are in the same boat there, in the passive role of waiting to be asked.

Certain questions arise about your work as an actress that I don't think puzzle critics about a male character, questions about being liked, or not liked, sympathetic or unsympathetic. Nobody sits there and says, 'Do I like Hamlet?', but in *All's Well That Ends Well* there are great outcries in the critical world about whether Helena is likeable or not. Shakespeare doesn't judge; he says, 'Here are these people. I've

14

given them each a motive and a background in human psychology. This is where they go and that's what they do.' Perhaps because I relate happily to women, instead of working from the 'objective' judgement of Helena—that she's an ambitious pushy woman—I wanted to work from within the character: her wants, desires, feelings, situation, her sense of herself. The performance, the fruit of the tree, happens because of the roots, and all the different heads in the audience see that fruit in their own ways. Critics have called my Helena 'deep', 'sincere', 'noble', 'brave', 'prissy', 'insufferable', 'priggish', 'go-getting'. It's the same person I've put on stage each night. That's why you can't be concerned with being liked, because of that huge spectrum of responses.

It didn't affect the way I played Helena, but my own self-censorship derives from wanting to please, wanting to be liked, feeling don't be unpleasant, don't be strident. Nobody will encourage you; the director won't say, 'She's really quite awful here, go for it.' That's something you have to decide and face out on your own. Often, for critics, if you're the heroine then you're automatically good and pure and vulnerable and sweet. Why should characters have to be Mrs Pure, or Mrs Evil? I'd love to be free to infiltrate some of those very particular observations you get in, say, Mike Leigh's work into a Shakespeare character. Daring to outface the puzzlement of critics and of the audience is something I haven't cracked but I'm braver than I was. Of course you don't want to block the communication by alienating: you try to find moments when you can show a nasty aspect, then redeem yourself the next moment. It's a luxury, to have a part so big you can show all the inconsistencies and shock or surprise people.

If you think of Ian Holm, or Denholm Elliott or Ian Richardson, they all have their own quirkiness, their own observations and details. You read what they do and you're fascinated: you communicate with them. They change; they're not predictable. That's what makes them last, and

15

you're never bored to watch them. There aren't that many equivalent women, because the demands of their parts are so much less. Perhaps women aren't seen as such diverse, rich and various human beings. Very often the woman's part has only one slight narrative point to make. That's true of all small parts, of course. If you're playing the cab driver nobody wants to know whether you've got acne. They just want to know what the fare was. But too often a woman's part is simply about, for instance, providing a hero who's in trouble with tension at home—providing more stress, more agony, for him to get out of. It's no good the actress playing the 'nagging wife' deciding to try and crack a joke, or throw a pillow at the hero's head, so you the viewer might think, I see, they've got a relationship, she's not always angry. They don't want that; they just want to see the pressure build up on the man. That's the shape of the narrative, and the narrative often concerns the man of action. And drama is things happening, action.

In smaller parts you're constantly coming up against limitations, and even when I'm not told about them I impose them on myself. Perhaps I've been spoilt by having my wings stretched—in the repertoire at the Royal Shakespeare Company I'm doing one huge part, then a lot of roles which are lovely, imaginatively rich characters, at the moment with many different challenges set up within them and so there's a lot to think about. In *A Midsummer Night's Dream* I play Helena, and the women in the play have a lot of force in the sense that they drive the scenes along. But quite often your part is that of a catalyst, like Lady Percy in both parts of *Henry IV*. She could be so many things—the brief is very wide—because who she is matters less than the light she throws on Hotspur. That's a really odd link you have to make. I don't mean that you're just looking at him and listening, but that you cut out all extraneous detail, and all the riches you could indulge, because what matters is the story line: you are sad because your husband's going to be hanged. You cut out thoughts like 'I'm going to be very brave today,' or 'I think I'll try her smiling at grief,' or cracking a bitter joke, or like a working-class woman who's going to survive and surprise you all. That's fine, it's a discipline that stops you being self-indulgent. A painter does one blob when he could do six. But it's hard when you've got all that energy there. Still, if I'm going to play somebody's wife, I'd rather do Shakespeare than *Z Cars*. It's just a little domestic situation, that Lady Percy and Hotspur scene. If you transported it to a modern script, the equivalent would be the policeman coming home with a burning problem about a murder he's got to solve. His wife would say, 'You haven't spoken to me for weeks, what the hell's wrong?' Then it would be resolved by an affectionate compromise. In this little scene in the first part of *Henry IV*, I go out there every night, and I feel tremendous. Because what I have to do is a forty-line speech, which contains only that domestic sentiment I've described, but uses rich imagery, poetic devices, humour, different tactics, energy focused first here and then there. The story's the same but the requirements of technique and physical range and stamina are so much bigger. That's why I went to the RSC, because Shakespeare gives you the opportunity to use your stagecraft, and that's something that's equal across the board. It's as difficult for a man to say that verse as it is for a woman. There's as much mind and heart to link up, as much technique and emotion—all those challenges set by the verse.

Television has opened up some good parts for women in the dramatizations of novels. I don't think things like situation comedies that reverse sex roles do a blind bit of good. They're amusement, but they don't go deep enough or make you think about serious issues. Something like *Testament of Youth* about the life of Vera Brittain does much more. When you read a novel, very often the novelist hasn't made a judgement about the heroine, sometimes hasn't even described her in any detail. It's a mind that's there; you are aware of a mentality and you go along with it. I love novels because you don't define in your own mind. They're shapeless, very imagined, without boundary. Of course, when a novel is

17

dramatized, and the actor is in the hands of the director—and all acting has less freedom in television—decisions have to be made. The character becomes this particular person. It could be very creative to try to be as amoebic as you imagine the character when you read about her in the novel, to change every time the camera is on you and show a different aspect of her.

Some male writers, like Ian McEwan, see women as other but not alien, not a threat. He put his female imagination into *The Imitation Game* which I was in on television. That part was completely central, a gift, though funnily more passive than a role in Shakespeare. The acting was watching, observing, and I could use a strength I probably have naturally. Other people pick that up in me, which is why they cast me. It's the kind of strength that watches, tries not to get fooled, preserves its privacy. You couldn't put that on stage; nobody would watch. But when the camera's glancing at your face every five seconds that quiet becomes strong.

There are so many assumptions in casting: so long as a woman's watchable, pretty, it doesn't matter who she is. All the care in the world will go into casting the male characters well. Yet there are so many chances now not to cast conventionally. I'm no beauty, but I got fan letters after *Imitation Game*. If you watch anybody on screen with the camera being empathetic and revealing what's going on in their mind, by the end of the film you've got to know them and love them. It's nothing to do with the shape of their nose.

The thrill of acting for me happens when my imagination has taken hold of something, and I can make it work by myself without anybody helping me. I'm definitely a calculator: I have to think it out before I go into rehearsal. There's not all that much spontaneity. That's partly the way I work, the sort of mind I have. I sometimes think I might get crushed, not dare to say anything or not be sure of my convictions, unless I come in with something to present. There is a social element in rehearsals, and you bring into the room the person you are; what you think they think of you, the fact you think they know more than you do, or that your status is low if you've got a small part, or you think it is. All those things get in the way, but if I'm armed with an awareness and am prepared, I won't get emotionally tongue-tied. If I went straight into the rehearsal room without any preparation I'd be steamrollered I think.

I may have sussed out that the leading guy wants to be seen as such and such, and I'll have thought over at home how I can make sure he gets his way and I get mine at the same time. There's an assumption in men, an arrogance that comes from the way the whole set-up feeds them, that their part is what matters most. As long as you serve their part, as an actress, then you're the best person they've ever worked with, because you're malleable. The play is assumed to be about him, not about this society, or all these people together, but about him. Lots don't do that, but lots do.

The way a scene ends up will often be because the person to speak up loudest was the guy, and his idea got in before yours, or you didn't have one at that point, and now you certainly don't because his has eclipsed yours. So you'll go along with it. I'm inhibited about taking initiatives in rehearsal, taking up time, keeping other people hanging around. Of course that isn't exclusively female, but so much of rehearsal is about assuming 'I have the right to ask this question, examine this possibility', however small your part. With a large part, you know you have to take that time. You feel wonderful but you've more fears, more responsibility.

In the 7:84 company I realized it was much easier to interrupt a woman than a man. The sheer energy and force behind the voice would make you hold back until there was a good moment to speak. I joined 7:84 because I had leanings toward Socialist ideas, although I thought that politics were something other people knew about. By getting into corners in pubs, and talking to individuals, the mystification went. I learned I had convictions, ideas, opinions. I never thought I had.

At school, you didn't have opinions, you learned the right

19

answers, and I was very much like that. If I had difficulty being heard as a woman, in 7:84, it was because there wasn't much in me to listen to at that stage. I can't say I was squashed or pushed into the background. But I learned that when something really struck me, when I felt so strongly that all fear and self-consciousness went, when there was something I was burning with, I could find the courage to speak. I never have any clear intellectual idea except when it's born from a feeling. Then my world changed, and I could see that in a company like the RSC I might be someone others might want to do some speaking for them. Given my present status within the company, there are certain things I can say, criticizing the directors perhaps, which others won't because they feel they can easily be replaced. I've got the younger-sister complex, I was always the follower rather than the leader, and I fit happily and snugly into that role. But there is a responsibility in a company, to speak out, and also to make people who've just come into the group feel at ease. You start being the hostess rather than the guest. You've got to take that on.

You've got to use what you've learned. I'm getting more extrovert because of the challenges of the work which I have to meet for my own pride. I'm intolerant now of people who say, 'I'm shy.' I want to say, 'Well so am I, but you can't be.'

I felt very small in status, very thrilled, very in awe, when I did my first important classical role—Ophelia. I'd longed to work at the Royal Court, and with that director [Richard Eyre]. I knew what he wanted of me. He's someone who uses what you are very well. I know now that half the job is in sussing out a director's expectations, and either going along with that, or working through it to something else. Then, I thought, now what does he want of me and I'll provide it. I knew he wanted a kind of imploding madness rather than a *tour de force*. I agreed with that. But I know that if I'd been free to explode in rehearsal and then bring it back I could feel prouder of what I did. I never took that plunge, releasing the running-wild imagination, anything goes, no confines. That stab. If I'd done that once in rehearsal and then held back.... I did that internal crack-up, that withering inside, to serve the play. It isn't about Ophelia, it's about Elsinore and that particular society.

I had huge strands of thought about her though she's so thin on paper. I related most to an R. D. Laing theme: having a very dominant father, being obedient, having a sense of self defined only by the men around you. When they crack up, or die, or change, the strings of the puppet are cut. So why should she sing and dance, or kick and thrust—that simplistic notion of sexual inhibition coming out in madness? It was much more like being stoned, quiet. I couldn't accuse Shakespeare of not having given me the opportunities. I don't think I took them.

With Nina in *The Seagull*, the conditions were set up for me to go as far as I could. The opportunities were there for me to take. And there was a moment in rehearsal when I thought 'Yes, cracked it!' It was exciting and the room went quiet. I never got that again, but maybe for the audience, seeing it for the first time, the moment was re-created, but because it was planned by then it couldn't take me by surprise. When you do something that takes you by surprise like that, it notches you up; it makes you grow and you never shrink back again. You've gone there, and you know you've gone there, and it's thrilling.

With directors, it's a two-way thing. They don't like people who hold back, or need to be coaxed and pushed. You've got to recognize the moment when they're saying, 'OK, so this happens, and that happens, and you've just done that, so now show me.' And they don't help you because they know that's your area, the bit they can't do for you. But they've given you all the clues, and if you don't take the chance now, it's your fault. I didn't know that in *Hamlet* but I did in *The Seagull*.

It's always better to assume there's a lot in someone, a character, and only weed it out at the last minute if it's necessary. I wanted to have a sense of humour in Helena in

All's Well, and there aren't many places where you can show that because she's in a desperate situation a lot of the time; she's not going to crack jokes very often. You might have to fight a director who doesn't want you to show that resilience, even though it's there in the character. You try to be a better person than you are yourself. It gets a bit religious sometimes! It can be very intense, going up there and being better, bigger, more human, braver, everything you wish to show a woman can be. If I have the opportunity, I really want to put that across. That's where my tiny little niche of changing the world is.

I've been working so hard recently, just drawing on myself all the time. 'Myself' is this limited bucket and I'm getting to the bottom. Because I haven't any other life. I've worked in these demanding companies, and I've loved it. But I think, I haven't travelled, I haven't had a love affair that's broken my heart, I haven't had a baby, or climbed Mount Everest, or worked in a shop. How can I keep my link with most people? That's the link you have to keep.

Travelling is my biggest loss. Sometimes when I've been travelling I've had a similar feeling to what I've experienced when acting, a feeling that you can burst through your own outline, redefine yourself. You're just behind your own two eyes when you travel; you don't look in the mirror; you forget what you look like; you learn. It feeds into what you are, how you think, and so into the choices you make when you're working on a part.

I've probably clouded my personal desires now by channelling them into other things. The point is that life feeds art, but you're still a growing, thinking person while you're working. I've learned through trying to move into someone else's imagination. I've broken my limits on myself, and I've noticed that my personality, my ways of thinking, ways of approaching things, have changed because of having to work through a character. You may start from a dream as a kid, that you can be anybody—Peter Pan, Huck Finn—and that hasn't gone from me. I still think there's nothing more real about who I am every day, my passport and my address, than there is about the fact that I'm Helena in *A Midsummer Night's Dream*. I can't quite see the difference. There is an obvious one: the life you have to lead. But you don't just build up a part from a point A which is you yourself. That point A shifts the more you work, and you begin to be able to say, for instance, 'Well—this character doesn't think like me. She doesn't even think, doesn't deliberate about what she does. She just does it.'

I've got more control of my work than I ever thought I would have. All actors are in a way the female in the relationship: they have to wait to be asked, invited, keep all they've got inside them until it's required. It's a very intangible kind of power. But I think now, instead of assuming as a woman, as an actress, that you've got very little power, you've got to say, 'Well just how far can I push it?' Pretend it's really up to you. It nags at me every night if I haven't really tried. Looking back, I see the interplay between what I chose to put forward on stage, what was picked up, my ability to assess what was being picked up, the ability of my colleagues to pick it up and go beyond it, the constant two-way relation that I have an absolute part in.

All I count as being a feminist is that, even if your individual lifestyle is all right, you identify every time a woman gets abused. I don't know where that comes from, but it's in that sense that I feel part of womankind. You keep your feet on the ground, you're one of everybody, but you're going to go beyond that, so that you can be special and unique without getting into a cult of personality.

If I can put on stage a woman who isn't confined by an image, or does slightly confuse the pigeon-holes, I feel encouraged. If I see someone else do that, I feel thrilled, excited, because I can identify. The men can't say, 'Got her number.' They have to treat you as a person. And you take them on a human journey every bit as much as Hamlet does. But you've got to preserve your links, your ordinariness—and your extraordinariness.

23

But will men like it?
Or living as a feminist writer
without committing murder

BRYONY LAVERY

1. *A Child of Destiny or Bryony, why are you keeping a file on Miss Popplewell?*

I was never going to be a writer.

I was absolutely sure what my career was going to be.

I was going to be a vet/nun/comedienne/artist/detective/ lifeguard and work on a Scarborough trawler.

Unfortunately I was wary of cows, horses and Alsatians, hideously unappealing in a wimple, shy of speaking in public, uncoordinated of hand and eye, cowardly, lazy and scared of all water particularly the sea.

So I filled in my time perfecting other skills.

From our Bedroom, my sister and I ran a skating school (Lino supplied by Skating School, bring Own Dusters for Feet).

After Dark my brothers and I went safe-cracking ... stealthily opening The Refrigerator, Father's Safe and Mother's *Private* Underwear Drawer WITHOUT Parents hearing.

The Boys' Bedroom was really a Detective Agency from which we observed everything that happened in the street. (Agency closed down after file on Miss Popplewell—teacher, single, retired, No. 21 Stockhill Street—fell into THE WRONG HANDS.)

In my childhood, meals, comfort, guidance and one or two smacks were provided downstairs, while upstairs, Imagination ran amok. It was a happy, workable arrangement. To stretch an analogy, it was like writing should be.

Meanwhile School taught Beginner's Reality, Intermediate Boundaries and Advanced Narrow Thinking.

School said Clever Girls became nurses, teachers or worked in offices. Oh, and incidentally ran homes too.

They did not become nuns/vets/comediennes/artists/detectives/lifeguards and they certainly did not work on trawlers. And I know that was back in the sixties, but when I was a teacher (Dear Reader, I did what School told me) the girls told me at eleven they were going to be airline pilots/army captains/cartoon artists and at sixteen left to become shop assistants/hairdressers and work in offices.

'Can't' and 'Don't' ruled everywhere except in the upstairs of our houses.

2. *The furniture develops a life of its own*

I started writing when I was a student—appearing in an experimental play written by a man and it was called *Furniture Revolts* ... and it was about ... well the title tells it all. I was playing the left arm of a sofa and as I stood still, left arm out (the person playing right arm of sofa stood with right arm out, the person playing middle of sofa ... it was a three-seater ... stood with both arms at side ... we were all female) watching as the armchair and the hatstand fell in love ... one male, one female ... I thought idly 'I can do better than this.'

So I wrote my first play.

Called *Of All Living* (again the title says it all) ... the Israelites fleeing from Egypt after the Plagues meet the Expelled from the Garden of Eden (happy family plus *female* snake) and ... well ... interact. Male Religious concepts with eight characters, six men and two women and the main parts were men and the two women's parts were the girl who

25

falls in love with the brave gritty hero and the brave gritty hero's wife ... would you say my consciousness was low, unawakened or what?

I was writing life as I knew it.

I wrote two more plays. More men than women. The best parts for men.

I wasn't a writer. Why? Because I wasn't being paid that's why.

We are what we are paid for. Having left college, I was a publicity assistant for Smith's Industries. It never occurred to me that I could make a living as a writer ... except in my wildest dreams ... which seemed to belong with The Skating School and The Safecrackers and The Detective Agency.

(Today I read in the newspaper that the average annual income of a playwright is £2000 ... so it seems that I still can't.)

Writing was a hobby Clever Young Women did at nights and at the weekend ... poems because they were short, novels because after all look at the Brontës and Jane Austen.

There were no Women Playwrights apart from the few exceptions which proved the rule that there were no ... I became a teacher.

3. *Fortunately for me, some other women start something called The Women's Movement*

The pages of the calendar flipped by.

Fortunately for me, while I had my eyes on the ground, others were looking around at the landscape.

Some started Fringe Theatre.

Others started The Women's Movement.

To put it bluntly, years after they built skyscrapers in New York, my ship docks on a new continent, which I call America, my New Found Land.

Two actors, Jessica Higgs and Gerard Bell, and I started a fringe theatre company because we were putting on a play and we were infinitely unknown and profoundly non-famous so the venue insisted we gave ourselves a collective group name and in a devil-may-care fashion we called ourselves Les Oeufs Malades ... which had everyone thinking we were art students who threw bad eggs at each other. We were not. We put on plays I had written.

In the next few years we put on *I Was Too Young At The Time To Understand Why My Mother Was Crying/Sharing, Grandmother's Footsteps, The Catering Service, Helen and Her Friends, Bag* and *The Family Album*. We toured the country in vans that broke down a lot, appeared sometimes before twelve people, argued with jobsworth caretakers and learned that 'venue has good lighting system' usually means four Anglepoise lamps.

I learned that just writing isn't enough. If you want to write the plays you want *and* have them produced and performed how you want, you also have to learn how to direct, how to raise money, deal with the Arts Council, talk people into putting your plays on in their theatre, talk to the press, talk to actors, talk to the audience afterwards and talk talk talk talk talk talk talk. I wrote plays because I believed I wrote better than I talked and when I'd written I learned that I had to learn to talk about what I'd written. The Great Ear and Two Typing Fingers discovered her Mouth. But the Mouth was avoiding the word 'Feminism'. I was full of ... 'No, I wouldn't call my work *feminist* as such ... it's about people, all people ... no, we don't advertise ourselves as *feminist*, because we don't want to preach, just to the *converted* ... while of course I sympathize with a *lot* of what people in the women's movement are saying ... half the world *is* men ... yes, of course I like men ... haha goodness me yes....' In the smallest meanest part of my mind, I felt that calling myself a feminist diminished me ... I was Me, the Great but As Yet Undiscovered, Unrecognized Writer. While I was grateful of course to Fervent Feminists, I was, well, you know, much *more* than that. (Yes, yes, I'm embarrassed too!) My plays at this time had more women than men in the cast. Both sexes were drawn sympathetically. The women characters were brave, intelligent, funny, loving, real and at the end of every play somehow ended up as the losers.

The critics, if they came (and in those years, as in all years, there were lots of revivals of Shaw, Shakespeare, Wilde to go to) mostly liked them. I was Promising.

4. *Female Trouble*

I wrote for Monstrous Regiment and The Women's Theatre Group. Gradually I became more and more impressed with the way they thought and believed. They did not start from a script ... they started from what they, the actors and administrators and directors, wanted to say. They worked so hard. And they were unashamedly feminist!

I'd also worked out how I liked to write; I like the excitement of writing very quickly. I wish I could type fast enough to write a play in the time it takes to play it out. *Then* the energy would be right, then the flow of ideas would be in the right dramatic curve, *then* the internal clocks of the characters would be ticking at the right speed. Being a two-finger typist I cannot work like that but I wanted the closest equivalent.

There is also a prevailing attitude that plays are scripts. They are not. A play is a wonderful nutty fruity cake (yes folks ... you can tell she's a woman writer ... she's using a *cooking* metaphor!) made up of the script, the director, actors, audience, technicians ... it's what happens the night we were *all* there for the performance.

Also, I realized that as a playwright I was a sort of job creation scheme. I could positively discriminate ... better parts for women, the best parts for women ... parts only for women!

Armed with these views, I set up Female Trouble.

Anne-Marie Davies, Caroline Noh, Lou Wakefield and I had three and a half weeks' rehearsal time, a definite opening time, a title and NO SCRIPT. The idea was to discover what we all wanted to say and do right there and then. (Insane huh?)

We realized that we wanted to present a positive female statement and we wanted our audience to have a treat, a laugh, a good night out.

One exercise we worked on. Called Yes But and Yes And. We tried two-way conversations wherein one person always answered with 'Yes ... but....'

'It's a lovely day.'

'Yes, but it might cloud over later.'

'I can sing.'

'Yes, but you can't dance.'

And conversely....

'It's a nice day.'

'Yes, and we're going to have a good time.'

'I can sing.'

'Yes, and I'd like to hear you.'

We all discovered that we found it is much easier to play 'Yes, But....' It was easier to doubt than believe, easier to say that things would go wrong than to say things would go right. We found we lived in a Yesbut world. We ended our show with a piece called *Yesbut Park*, where the woman lived in a park, created by a god who said live in my park but don't walk on the grass, but don't pick the flowers but don't step out of line. The women are saved by a Yesand Angel whom they discover writing golden graffiti in the park toilets. She tells them to get out there and say 'Yes and' to everything....

I realized how much of my work had been set in the Yesbut Park. My women characters were brave, intelligent, funny, loving, real ... *yes but* at the end of every play they ended up as the losers. I wanted them out of that park.

5. *The Piltdown Woman—an archaeological discovery*

I lost interest in valiant losers.

With four women this time—Kay Adshead, Donna

Champion, Claire Grove and Sue Rogerson—I set out to produce 'an unusual thriller'. The unusualness came from there being no villains, the women were fighting against their own deepest fears. These fears came from the thrillers they read. They were helped out of their fear-prisons by a gaoler who became a guide once they thought positively about escaping. And they escaped. As with *Female Trouble*, the ending was joyous.

On stage at least, women were not the losers.

I became increasingly aware of the distorting-mirror effect of many of the stories in my head from childhood on.

The story of Circe ... a wicked witch on her own enchanted island who turned innocent sailors into pigs ... surely from what I know of women's characters ... wasn't it more likely that here was a woman running her own island rather well, harassed and bothered by sailors abroad for a good time who *behaved* like pigs?

I collected stories for *For Maggie, Betty and Ida* for Topfloor Productions. In one story ... *The Piltdown Woman* ... archaeologists discover a woman's body in a walled-up cell. They cut her open and discover to within a year the time of her death, that she had once broken her foot, and that she had perfect teeth. What they fail to uncover is the layer upon layer of stories in her, the stories that make up what she is. If we continue to hear and see stories in which we are valiant losers, that will be what we are made of.

6. *The Great Theatre Museum War*

It's time for a war.

At the moment The Theatre seems too much like a great museum run by male curators. The glass exhibition cases are opened up and historic exhibits taken out and shown to us all, if we can afford the entrance fee. Theatre is about the living, museums about the dead.

There are too many Dead Writers being taken out of their glass cases.

There are far too many good women actors for the amount of space in those glass cases.

There is too much to say today to listen to the voices of the museum ghosts.

This is the complaining section.

I am tired of my role as cleaner in this museum. Most of the rubbish is dropped by men.

I rest on my broom and imagine....

Imagine a British Theatre scene where there is no Shakespeare Memorial Theatre, no Shavian revivals, not another production of *The Importance of Being Earnest* ... all play-scripts are in the reference section ... you can read them, you can refer to them, you can adore them ... but you've got to get out there and do something *new*, something *now* ... how many cast lists then would you read with ten parts for men, two for women ... one the girl who falls in love with the brave gritty hero and the other the brave gritty hero's brave gritty mother?

(And yes I *know* Shakespeare's wonderful and has a lot of terrific speeches and has such a lot to say to us even now but I don't care I tell you ... I'm far more interested in that big fat bag of gold being spent on LIVING playwrights. These dead playwrights are working too cheaply for us who have to do more than lie in a grave all day to compete with.)

Imagine a Theatre for Women somewhere in Warwickshire, by a river, well subsidized....

Imagine a National Theatre somewhere in London, say, by a river, well subsidized, putting on NEW plays....

I pick up my broom and get back to work.

7. More Female Trouble—but will men like it?

I've been a child of destiny. I've been furniture. I've been not really feminist. I've been the Yesand Angel in the Yesbut Park. I've been buried. I've been the cleaner in the Theatre Museum.

Now I've come out.

I am a lesbian feminist writer.

or in other words

I am the writer of *More Female Trouble*.

or in other words

I am passionately dedicated to the rediscovery of women's strength through positive theatrical presentation.

or in other words

I chose the theatre as the place in which I am best equipped to fight for the world I want.

More Female Trouble suggested a withdrawal by women from a world which condoned male violence, which condoned rape, which condoned war. It suggested that it was not the task of women to change men. That is the task of men.

At every interview I gave, the second or third question was 'But do you think men will like it?'

That is not why I write. Not any more.

I had a skating school once. It was mine. I ran it. I want it back. It afforded me great pleasure. When the men have learned to skate properly without digging in their blades they may be invited back.

Oh, one more thing.

I don't think I've mentioned this.

I love to write.

Let me recommend it to you.

Box of tricks

DI SEYMOUR

When I was about seventeen and at a girls' boarding school, we had a very batty but marvellous, imaginative music teacher, who was fiendishly ambitious for us. She used to put on very over-ambitious productions, and I was involved in two of them, both operas. I had a musical involvement in the first, *Dido and Aeneas*—an obvious choice as it was written for a girls' school—and I played a courtier or something. But the important one for me was *The Magic Flute*. She did it in a greatly abbreviated form. And in the middle of doing A levels, and music exams, and presumably other activities, I put together the sets, such as they were, and costumes, and painted the scenery and sang Papageno as well.

It was a ridiculous undertaking but at the time I thought it was wonderful. I wasn't clear in my mind from the enjoyment of the experience whether I had liked the visual aspects or the performance most. The performance was responded to more directly; I was on stage, and people came up afterwards. The designer is a quieter person in that situation, more in the background. But it was that particular experience that made me think I wanted to be involved in all that in some way. There was a sense of everybody doing something, all together, in order to make this huge event to which people came, and enjoyed themselves. It seemed as if the whole school suddenly drew itself together.

I found what happiness I did at school at that time, in the sixth form, when the natural competitiveness became about using your brains and having ideas, and not about having the right sort of boyfriend or liking the right sort of record. For the first time I had something to offer that gave people pleasure. All I did as a set for *The Magic Flute* was a load of flats about four foot wide, all angled backwards. That was the full extent of my idea. I think there was a backdrop and we painted it like a forest for the world of the Queen of the Night and Papageno. Then we turned it all round, and it was painted in reds and oranges, with suns, and Egyptian columns and hieroglyphics. Just that, turning it around and it becoming something else, I thought was wonderful. There were a lot of people involved, girls making costumes and mothers and fathers helping as well, so presumably I must have put things down on paper, but I can't remember doing it.

I sort of came out, became someone who really had achieved something. In terms of my peers up to then I was completely out of it. I never felt I could participate in the field of sport in any way. I had no social success, and only a moderate academic success, but that wasn't admired so I didn't aspire to it. It was the first time I had a chance to shine in any way, even though in reality the whole idea of being artistic was frowned upon in the school. The girls were concerned with social success and, as far as the teachers were concerned, in the sixth form you were after academic success. The headmistress told my mother I ought to go to the Bar. That was palpably ridiculous and fortunately my mother laughed. It wasn't what I wanted to do. It was a great disappointment to the school that I went to the art school not a university.

Design is two separate worlds, one of which is private and one of which is very public. The actual process of designing is done almost completely alone, and if you're freelance very fequently in your own home. You work with the director in the brief periods when you're discussing the work, but the real achievement of the design happens alone. Then later, you become a very public person in the middle of a number of different processes: the actors and director in rehearsal, the carpenter's workshop, the wardrobe, the production office, different groups and disciplines.

The good moments, when you're on your own and the design actually comes, are very extraordinary and completely private. It's glorious when your imagination becomes concrete. First of all there's the excitement of just getting ideas, which I find happens very fast in short bursts. You begin to see the characters on the stage, and what they look like, to see what the feeling of the piece is. That all happens in your head, and then comes this awful jumping-off-the-top-of-a-diving-board feeling, when you have to transmit the ideas to paper. There is always a great sense of compromise and disappointment because the things that are floating round in your head are always greater than the reality. That's quite aside from the practical disciplines of the circumstances: money, limitations of resources. What Michelangelo's idea for the *Last Judgement* was and what he actually came up with must, even for him, have been something of a disappointment. It always is, in any artistic process.

Designing a show is like solving a Chinese puzzle. First you get the flurry of ideas, then the nasty bit when you think 'Oh god, how can I make that happen?' Then there's the rather dreary process of beginning to think in more concrete terms. Very gradually all the pieces start to come together. When that happens, you're not thinking imaginatively, but practically. 'If I had a flat there, and then turned it, and as it turns the actors are walking through, and lights came up here and sound....' It's as if you're describing a wonderful box of tricks, a puzzle that's beginning to move in its own way. That's very satisfying, because at that stage there's every possibility it really will happen; that what you're thinking of, and beginning to make with your hands as a model, is going to happen on a stage in front of people. I find I get so I have to jump around, move, because I get giddy with excitement.

The classic moment of the public phase in your work comes when you're standing at the back of the auditorium, the show's working well and people are moved, enjoying it,

35

yet it's been taken from you in a way. It isn't just your baby, it belongs to everybody else as well. It feels like a sort of bereavement. In the end you do have to hand your design over to the actors and they have to make it their own. That's why designers get drunk on first nights, because it's a bit unbearable, the handing over of all that private imaginative world.

Recently, working at Exeter, I had a very good experience. I had designed a simple set in some ways, but the way it was solved, put together, brought satisfaction to the people I was working with. They got excited at the thought of how it was going to work out. They started to have ideas about it themselves and so it flowered into a co-operative piece of work. There was no sense of bereavement in that at all. It was very satisfying. It's marvellous when a carpenter, a person of immense practicality, gets a buzz out of a design, and says, 'Well, it's going to be difficult, but I think for your design it's worth the effort, worth the extra work to do this and this.'

You can work on a design which, purely as design piece is undemanding, but what it's about and what it's for, what it's saying, you feel very passionately about. *Diary of a Hunger Striker* was an example of that. It was an interesting thing to design: taking a real place, the prison of Long Kesh, and then taking it a step further, to a theatrically satisfying concept of prison. It's an interesting synthesis, the literal reality of the place and the evocation of a very modern prison. I wanted to suggest endlessly long, grey, institutional corridors, kept immaculately clean, and at the same time suggest a process through the play—it's not just the world of prison but also that of government ministers, and statements in the House, and the press. In the middle of all that is this shit-lined little hell-hole with these two very strong men standing there stark naked.

It's not glamorous, and it doesn't make anything like the demands that, say, Shakespeare does, of having to create a whole world. It has very defined limits. But I have a strong commitment to the way the play works politically, and that it's being done now, and that people come out of the play and argue about what has happened and what will happen in Northern Ireland. That has its own special joy. You can do something which is fascinating in terms of textures, fabrics, colour and atmosphere, but which in the end doesn't say very much about anything. On the first night you can think 'What does it all add up to? Not very much.' Those can be two completely different processes, and they can have their own particular satisfactions and limitations.

It's important for me to identify with the statement of a piece, though it can be very uncomfortable. As I was making the final model for *Diary* the announcement came on the radio of the guardsmen being blown up in Regent's Park. My wonderful private world of making artistic things on the stage and the reality outside converged most uncomfortably. And I had to think, does that mean we must do something different? And in fact we did. Originally, at the back of the set we had banners that looked almost like fragments of walls in Belfast, and we had wanted them to be just Republican. In response to the alarming feelings we had about the bombing, we thought we should take one step back and have the banners represent the full spectrum. In the middle was the announcement that's made about phoning the police if you know anything, the exhortation for people to betray, the voice of the security forces. Then to the right we had the Republican slogans and pictures, and to the left the Protestants'. So in a sense we took a more objective view. That's what we felt we should do.

As a designer, you're in the middle of a lot of different theatre processes. Technical people can make you feel on your own—a creature of dreams and notions—and that they are the down-to-earth ones who will actually make it happen. I think male designers sometimes experience aggravation from the women, and female designers from the men in the team. There's the old trick of blinding you with science. I know one or two male designers who are terrified at walking into a wardrobe, because it is generally regarded as the female part of the theatre, the preserve of skilled women, and men think they're going to get pushed around, told things aren't possible, can't be done. Certainly I've experienced all that terror walking into a workshop.

You can feel very doubtful about the whole of what you're doing, because they don't say, 'I don't like what you're doing.' They just say 'This won't work,' or 'We can't afford that.' If something can't be made to work that's a reality and one's got to deal with it, but there can be a sense in which people don't want to listen to what you're trying to achieve, don't want to stand behind it and push along with you.

You always feel you ought to have more expertise than perhaps you have, that you should have a grasp of carpentry and lighting and so on. But you can't know all the trades and disciplines of the theatre. It would take a lifetime to learn them. You're a designer, not a half-baked carpenter. But I've had it pulled on me by male technicians, the implication that because I'm a woman I don't know about certain technical aspects and I bloody well ought to, and if I did it would be very much easier. That's nonsense. If I know my job and they know theirs we can make it work.

I can remember once wanting to do something with a structure, and the technicians saying it couldn't be done, that it wouldn't swing round the way I wanted, or it wouldn't be as smooth and well oiled as it needed to be. I knew that if they'd put their energy and commitment and creativity behind it they'd've found a way to make it work. It isn't a matter of going in there and saying 'This is what I want,' and then making it work. It's a negotiated thing. You say, 'How are *we* going to do it?' That's when it's difficult, when people won't respond to the 'we', to the sense of the process being a synthesis between someone who's dealing with ideas and someone who's dealing with practical realities, of the two being brought together in a creative partnership.

A lot of technicians are never treated as creative people, their opinions are not sought in that way. Perhaps some designers are under the impression that they can get their way by not having to explain themselves, not consulting. I think my natural fondness for feeling it is a collective process works very well. I don't want to feel egocentric, controlling, and I feel a satisfaction when everybody has contributed to the end result. There are ways of building things that I don't know about—I don't build things every day—but a small detail a carpenter will add can completely transform something, make it easier and lighter, more flexible. That may be one reason why there are a lot of good women designers: maybe women don't need to feel they've got absolute control. In a way the designer is supposed to be in an executive role, leading the team in the construction of this wonderful thing, and I think there are some designers who don't like to be told what to do. In fact people don't tell you what to do; they tell you what *they* would do, and you negotiate around that.

The relationship with actors comes into its own in the fitting room. I always find it unsatisfying, because the timing is wrong. You're often having to design costumes completely separately from the actors. Sometimes that's all right: if twenty-five actors are walking on as courtiers, getting into in-depth discussion with each individual isn't going to get you anywhere. What you're doing with them is making an overall visual statement with a group of people. More interesting is the synthesis between how a costume looks and how it is worn, between what you've designed and what the actor feels. But it's very difficult to bring it together, because by the first day of rehearsal the ball is already rolling: fabrics are being bought, resources committed. I always resent the feeling that you almost have to talk the actors into believing that it's all going to be wonderful, into having to trust you. It's unsatisfying because it rules out their creative feeling towards the costume.

It's fascinating when I do have the chance to talk very generally to the cast on the first day of rehearsal, and then again a few days later when they're beginning to get the 'smell' of the characters, do rough sketches, talk again—a

39

very gentle, very slow growing together of your ideas from the outside and theirs from the inside. For example, when I was doing *Schweik in the Second World War*, I was able to have an hour-and-a-half fitting with Michael Williams who was playing Schweik. At the end of it, the costume looked as if he'd lived in it for twenty years. He tried things out, explored—very imaginative things, like trying on dozens of caps. There's no way you could find out by doing hundreds of lovely drawings. It was a matter of getting lots of hats and putting them on his head, and him saying, 'Yes that's really crazy, let's try that one.' On the first day of rehearsal, to be sitting there with your paper, in the same way an actor is, in the same situation, is ideal: you discover it together.

I think being a woman may give you a skill for finding out if an actor's being 'difficult', or whether he or she needs help and support. I remember dealing with an actress who had a reputation for being difficult, and she had a massive central role. She wouldn't stop talking at fittings: they lasted for hours and hours, bottles of wine, they went on terribly late. The wardrobe staff I was with felt I was being given the runaround and they probably despised me for it. But on the first night she came to me and said, 'I think your costumes look wonderful and you've been so kind.' And you think, if someone's saying that, they needed that bit of support— which wasn't so difficult to give—a bit more time, a few more glasses of wine. It isn't all costume: you can make it look wonderful from the shoulders down but it's still got to look good from the shoulders up. And she did that—when she wanted to look wonderful she did, and when she wanted to look strange and batty she did that too. And I helped her get on the stage and do it.

In the relationship with the director, in the early stages it's just you and him or her, looking at sketches and models together. Then you launch out into this very public process when it becomes very difficult to reach your director because he or she is in demand by other people. The early stage is nice: what the director has to concentrate on is the design—

with you. There's also a very open, negotiable area as to who's running the show at that stage. You're both learning the play, finding out, doing research, reading. Some directors get twitchy if you find a good piece of research instead of thinking how good that you're not just thinking about flats and drapes. If you're engaging with the play intellectually, discovering depths and angles, fresh views, directors can suddenly cut off and not want to hear. I think a director who wants total control isn't using the designer properly. Designers have changed, very fast and quite recently, and I like to think I've been part of that change. Designers are no longer people who just decorate; we analyse, we go through a very precise intellectual process. I'm sure they did that in the past—but the way the job is viewed has changed. So it's frustrating to work with a director who doesn't want to involve the designer's intellectual capacities.

The directors I've worked best with have either been very demanding, or absolutely hopeless. If they're hopeless they leave you with a tremendous trust: you plough on, fire on all guns, and come up with good work. Or you get someone who may be heavy-handed but makes you go for it, jump through the hoops and really stretch yourself: it might be rough going but it's very stimulating. I enjoy that, but more in retrospect than at the time! You kick and scream and hate it. I remember one director—I thought at the time he was being horrid—saying, 'You can go further, more, more.' Then he said, 'I'm only saying this because I know you can go there,' which is a great trust in your abilities, and that's got to be stimulating.

There are differences between working with a director who's a woman, and a director who's a man. The fact that women are so good at functioning on an equal basis, woman to woman, can be so much of a relief that we tend to go in the other direction and lack the grit to say, 'Go further, go for that, go for broke.' Sometimes you feel the full potential isn't being recognized, that by being afraid to ask for that bit more a woman director may be losing out on something that has to

41

be found by both of you. That's in the early stages. The skill of being more candid and more honest, the lessening of status games that I've experienced with women directors, is all to the good in that later, more collective stage.

If you've really put your head down and pushed in that early private stage, when it's a battle with the imagination and the heart and the mind, it's amazing how much smoother the path is later on. You know you've gone as far as you possibly can and so the director will go into the next phase, into rehearsal, with the play really beginning to form in the mind. It begins to have colour, and texture, and if that is really solid, I'm sure they must feel they're standing on something very dependable.

The area I find most difficult is lighting. I don't know enough about it. It may be significant that it is almost throughout the theatre a male preserve. It is the area where I've found the one or two who won't respond to the 'we' approach. They want to make it their baby. Recently I worked with a lighting designer like that, and I think in the end it impaired his work because he didn't relate to the thing as a whole. The only way through I could have found would have been to say something like 'Do this because I know it will fucking well work.' I couldn't use that rather shabby rank-pulling because I didn't know enough.

What I was taught by my teacher, Percy [Margaret Harris, of Motley], a woman and a very good designer, and still one at a great age, is that you do give people the benefit of the doubt, you do listen out for what their needs are, what they're trying to tell you, trying to contribute. But if it reaches the point where their obstruction is going to compromise the result—which after all in the end has your name on it—you put the boot in. The final card—and I once heard Percy use it—is 'It's going to be that way because I bloody well designed it.' I've almost never had to say that because most people are in it because they have a passion about theatre. A carpenter would make more money in almost anything but theatre, and work much less hard.

The responsibility when you work in a big institution like the Royal Shakespeare Company can be scaring. The RSC has a massive reputation to support, so a very glaring eye will be on anything you do. It's got to live up to the things that surround it and precede it. That helps in some ways; it sharpens you up. But what I've felt, because there's so much going on, so many shows at the RSC, is fear that I won't be able to make the imaginative leap, that the work will get small and frightened. When you're drawing or making there is a bit of your brain that works itself loose and goes free. I always listen to the radio to distract it. You're working away ninety-nine per cent absorbed but the other one per cent flowers into anxiety. 'This is the best opportunity you've had for six months.' 'They've done this play ten times before—better.' 'Who do you think you are anyway?' All those things crowd in, and it's also difficult not to think in terms of leagues, with the RSC as Division 1. You tell people you've worked there, and there's no doubt about it they do take note, beyond what you've actually done or how good it was—just that fact is your England cap.

When you get to the second stage, your path is better oiled than in smaller set-ups. You get the absolute delight of having more resources, and resources mean people, very skilled people, the best in the business. That's a joy. They take your ideas and make and create them so well. Because I feel a certain confidence about working with people, putting myself across, and getting a sense of commitment to the design, I feel I can use the opportunity to the full. In an organization like that, the acid test—what makes people excited—is whether the thing is artistically right, is beautiful, or magnificent, or overwhelming. That it's well made and well done everybody assumes. The practical side must be answered for and worked out, but the weight is on the other side, what they want is for you to be a good artist.

I do find that self-doubt is often more draining than the healthy questions any artist should have. The feeling, when you're doing a show at the RSC, that someone's done it seven hundred times before, saps you terribly, whereas that situation should be marshalling the best in you. In fact I marshal the best despite the doubts but they take a lot of energy. I experience them as finding it very difficult to think straight, feeling mentally very foggy, it being hard to concentrate on new ideas. Partly that's the way you work. You don't think 'I'm going to do this, then this.' You work conceptually, and you should allow ideas to leap out from surprising parts of your brain, or in the middle of the night and you put them down on a fag packet. But I think the self-doubts add to the fog in an unhelpful way. If you can clear your mind of all that it's-going-to-be-boring or when-they-did-it-before-it-was-better stuff, you probably will find a less boring solution, be more imaginative.

I haven't had to see myself very much in competition with other designers—you don't sit in a room with others with your portfolio, being 'up for' something in the way actors do. They have to deal bravely with the feeling of not being right, being too fat or too thin, all the time, and they're probably more relaxed about it than designers. The contact tends to be personal, and you always like to think you're the only one they phoned! Sometimes you watch a show, and think 'That's so bad, I could do better' and you feel shabby about thinking it, or 'That's marvellous,' and then, in brackets, 'I feel really envious because I don't think I could do that even if I had the chance.' That's naked ambition. You're just trying to have a nice evening out, and all these dark uncomfortable feelings are coming up. I remember when I was doing *The Winter's Tale*, a designer appeared, and said 'It looks marvellous Di—I'm so angry!' That was very nice, a very honest compliment. A lot of women get anxious about competitive feelings, and think they're lousy, butch and horrible. But they do help you, give you the strength and spirit to get on and do it, do something bigger next time.

I sometimes feel that I am slightly typecast to the small-scale, so that means the bigger scale has become a bait. There's also status involved: if you can handle the massive, the operatic, it smacks of facility, flexibility and scope. What matters is what might actually happen in reality and what I could do well. I just wouldn't do *Orpheus in the Underworld* well. I think it's incredibly silly and trivial. I'm not interested in doing something that's pure visual statement for effect. I think I'm good with content and that's one of the most important aspects of the experience. You allow yourself fantasies like 'Shall I ever do *The Ring* at Bayreuth?' But the real fantasy for me would be to do a cracking, wonderful feminist opera at the National Theatre. A combination of things that I care passionately about, that are part of my experience, and yet would demand a big-scale, bravura, epic, very visual and exciting design. That's the real fantasy. It's not just about getting into a posh theatre and getting a big fee and lots of money to spend. I count myself fortunate in that my career has related to my abilities and my feelings. When I got breaks, they were on a scale I could handle. My first opera wasn't *Orpheus in the Underworld*; it was *The Beggar's Opera*, a chamber work, with very strong characterization in it—all things I know very well.

There are dangers in finding your work all-absorbing. You can somehow lose touch with yourself. You can become Di the designer and Di the private person. Inevitably, if there's any kind of damage done, it's being done in my private life, in the sense that I haven't fought for that in the way I've fought for my work. I sense there are areas of neglect in the non-working part of my life, not sacrifice, but a sort of thoughtlessness, being over-casual about taking care of the self.

That private person's relation to the work is important, because this business defines success and failure all too vividly. You have your work written about, talked about, displayed; and it's terribly important in the end that you have your own ideas about how you're succeeding, that it's your own, not other peoples' assessment. I want to work out my full life as a human being, as a fully-fledged woman, as a woman artist. And I've got to do that in a world which picks people up and drops them very readily.

Di Seymour

There's always the wonderful, ever-hopeful feeling that the show you're just about to start is going to be terrific. It's going to be the best design, and everyone's going to go 'Wow, I've never seen anything like that in all my life!' Of course when you get down to it, it isn't quite like that. But the best reason for me to continue to be a theatre designer is that I think it's simply the thing I do best. I can't think of any other area of visual art that feels so right.

Directions

PAM BRIGHTON

Years and years ago, shortly after I'd first met Buzz Goodbody, we sat down with a couple of bottles of whisky and talked non-stop for about ten hours. It is a memory I will always cherish, one of those rare, if not unique, occasions where it is worth articulating every nuance of one's experience because what one is hearing in reply is such an uncanny similarity of feeling and experience. I have never been able to repeat that with anyone else. With most other directors the antagonisms loom larger than the shared experience, and if ever there was a profession designed to cultivate an antagonist nature, directing plays is prime: forced as one is to define in the most precise way possible how people experience reality, every day of one's working life. Laced with fear and intellectual conceit as the exercise is prone to be, it becomes all too easy to attack others engaged in the same work who appear to be producing only a muddle-headed facsimile of it.

Consequently, the friends within my working life tend to be the writers, actors and designers I work with, rather than other directors—a fact I regret deeply: I'm sure there's something pretty unnatural about not having a dialogue with someone doing the same job as yourself. I scrounge stories of other directors' working methods from the people I work with, but so appalling has the divisiveness in the theatre become that the expectation is always that you want to hear the bit where they fall on the banana skin. One spends a lot of time working in the theatre battling against the spiritual weariness that overtakes one in the constant realization that

50 per cent of all theatre talk is recrimination and character assassination.

Now the $64,000 question: how much does my professional isolation have to do with the fact that I'm a woman? Do all those chaps have a tremendously supportive brotherhood going on, the way forward clear, well worn by inspiring predecessors? Strangely enough, I never felt myself short of female prototypes. Having grown up on a housing estate in Bradford, by the time I was sixteen I knew one thing: I wanted to work in the theatre, thanks largely to an extraordinary man called Mike Walker, who founded a group called Group Theatre which attracted a very bizarre collection of people—among them Barry Hanson, Nick Simmonds, Edward Peel, Stephanie Turner—people who would never have contemplated such an exotic notion as the theatre without him. I can't remember how I became involved, perhaps I fancied Eddie Peel. Anyway, Group Theatre introduced me to this remarkable way of earning a living that was quite beyond any expectations I'd held of work up until that point. The second great certainty I had was that I was a Socialist. Brought up in a family that still held the odd great aunt and uncle who had known Keir Hardie and dedicated their energy and youth to creating the Labour Party, I was taught politics were quite simply about the class struggle. I was also told, with an uncomprehending sadness, that the Labour Party had let them down—they'd not read Marx or understood why. This expressed itself in a deep suspicion of the south and its implicit corruption, and anyone who went down there was swallowed up willy-nilly by material greed and the need to play at silly middle-class practices. Why I became obsessed by running that particular sword of Damocles, I'm not sure.

Neither of these obsessions, which formed themselves dimly into the shape of arming my class with theatrical weapons, had any reality until I stumbled upon an article in the library about Joan Littlewood. I couldn't quite believe it. Here it was in one person: Socialist, theatre director and a woman—a notion to hitch one's dreams to. I was seventeen and she crystallized my fantasies into a possible reality. I've only met her once; she came to talk at the London School of Economics about fun palaces. I found her overwhelmingly eccentric, sitting there surrounded by classy Marxist students who patronized her like mad. I'd wished she'd been more socially acceptable. It was to be years later before I realized that to be a woman who holds on to a singular vision with passion is practically equivalent to appearing to most people to be crazy, perverse and rather frightening. Strangely enough though, my infatuation with Littlewood has come full circle: in a fairly black mood one day I picked up the *Guardian* arts page, anticipating the usual series of news and views I didn't agree with, when there was Littlewood's obituary for Harry H. Corbett—brilliantly written, so sad, so perceptive, the most wonderful piece of writing I'd read about the theatre for ages. And yet, is she honoured? Is her contribution to English theatre revered? You'll not catch Melvyn Bragg making ninety-minute documentaries about her—she just might tell him where to stick his cultural opinions.

But back to the point of naïve optimism: the world is a possible enterprise of which one could be a part, period. I was hugely lucky shortly after leaving university, when I still didn't know how to turn the ambition of being a theatre director into becoming one, in meeting Jane Howell and beginning work at the Royal Court as an assistant director. Jane confirmed my feeling that if one was ballsy and determined enough there was no problem about being a woman director. The period of all this, of course, is important. It was the late sixties and early seventies—pre-feminism. I'd read Doris Lessing's *The Golden Notebook*, so I knew how important that kind of detailing of contemporary female experience was, but I didn't see my perceptions as hinging on the fact of being a woman. The atmosphere all around London was one of such heady social change that one quite sincerely believed that all social, emotional and sexual barriers were in the process of being eroded. I had a baby

when I was 23, quite confident that it would in no way inter-
fere with my work, confident that I was part of a generation
that could easily resolve such paltry domestic problems. The
Court at that period was run by William Gaskill, and I
couldn't have had a more wonderful nurturing pad. It was a
context in which creative ideas were at a premium and where
the theatre encouraged my cultural independence at all times.
In any other context my class and my sex might well have
proved such stumbling blocks that I would have soured
before I'd learned. As it was, my confidence in, and commitment to, my work developed before I had to tangle with the
ugly realities of English theatrical life.

But that period ended with Bill leaving the Royal Court
and I had to face the market-place. For the first time I
was faced with the reality that I was totally unlike anyone
else who did my job—with a couple of notable exceptions
(Buzz Goodbody and Sue Todd), they were all men. And,
of equal consequence, the majority of them were from
Oxbridge, implicitly schooled in the art of career building,
irreversibly confident of their abilities and consequent in-
evitable rise in the cultural hierarchy. Essentially at one with
reality, they might carp a bit at its more obvious amoral
excesses and stupidities but that air of ironic detachment
gave them a relationship to it that has always eluded me. I
began to learn that to be serious about something left one in
constant danger of being regarded as potentially naïve,
boring, stupid or all three. Manoeuvring my way around
England's cultural institutions with sufficient dexterity to
support myself and my child began to feel like walking
through a minefield. I pulled the duvet over my head and
went to bed for three months, taking with me everything by
or about Brecht—the only glimmering of salvation I could
find.

I got the Beaumont award for my production of *Ashes*, and
whilst generally being touted as an exciting young director
about town, I was in fact sitting in a corner of my room,
entirely stymied. To what extent did I attribute this alien-

ation to being a woman? Not a great deal. I understood that the whole cultural apparatus of the country, like everything else, was in the grip of the Oxbridge mafia, whether male or female. They seemed to me pretty committed to business as usual, whatever charade they might put out about new ideas and cultural change. I've never really believed the idea that there is something fundamental to being a woman that makes you inherently less conservative and keen to hang on to what you've got than men.

After three months' contemplation I came back—as I always do after a crisis—to my original inspiration for working in the theatre in the first place: to create theatre for working-class audiences. Infinitely more easily said than done, given the structures of artistic patronage. One of the main experiences that confirmed for me that this was right and not a remnant of adolescent whimsy, was a production I'd done at the Royal Court Theatre Upstairs of Barry Reckord's *Skyvers*. It's an account of the violence and futility felt by a group of kids at the end of their school careers. They feel all they have been equipped for is unemployment, dead-end jobs and delinquency. (In 1971 this was a fairly staggering social revelation!) We'd played it at the Court to school matinées, working to get kids from the classic, tough areas of east and south London in. The kids were astounded by it. Never had they seen their experience respected and articulated on a stage before, the whole process that goes on in our society that makes large groups of kids delinquent in their heads. *Skyvers* was a tiny drop that attempted to work against that tide. The play was successful enough to transfer to the Roundhouse. The first schools' matinée was over-booked: seven hundred 14- to 15-year-olds, ready to tear the building apart. The actors felt as if they were being thrown to the lions, terrified to begin. Within five minutes you could have heard a pin drop. It stayed that way for two and a half hours, that profound and rapt attention which, as a director, you hunger for. 'Profound' is an easy adjective to use. But what does one mean by that quality of communication that rarely takes place in a theatre, but which has to be constantly hungered after?

I think I always start from the assumption that our society as it exists now is a pretty poor excuse for our society as it could be, and the way we become human is by struggling to transform reality into something which more fully expresses the extraordinary potential people have. I loathe plays that tart up accepted realities as something to be satisfied with. Those tinny responses that are elicited on the assumption of humanity's inveterate backwardness and seek to trap people even more tightly into the circumference of their lives. *Skyvers* didn't do that. By confirming the reality of the violent responses of the kids to a world that would only make them eat shit, it confirmed that those violent responses, which other people sought to describe as their worst, were in fact the ones that made emotional and social sense.

It was the experience of *Skyvers* that led me to the Half Moon, a struggling community theatre in Aldgate. I persuaded them to let me do Brecht's *St Joan of the Stockyards*—my favourite play, I think. It's the only play I know that really attempts to illuminate those dynamics that urge us to accumulate wealth and power despite an awareness of the social implications. It was the first Brecht play I'd worked on and it confirmed for me a feeling that he is the towering genius of our epoch. I often wonder if someone of comparable intellectual stature would even bother with the theatre nowadays—seeing it as about as much use as the lace industry to the transmission of ideas.

I was involved with the Half Moon for three years, the last as artistic director, moving down to the East End and devoting the most lunatic amount of time to it. It was without doubt the most productive and gratifying period of my life. Up until that point I'd had a lot of ambiguity about my working personality, becoming almost Jekyll-and-Hyde-like—dominating and able at work but occasionally cowering back into parodies of female passivity when outside it. But at the Half Moon I felt sufficient moral conviction in what I was about not to feel embarrassed by my own energy. The East End, once I had got to know it, became a very warm world to exist in. There were some initial tensions linked with being a single woman. Was I one of those sexual radicals who'd be wrecking marriages, jumping in and out of beds, an easy lay? Once it became clear that I was a respecter of marriages I went on to make some really good friends.

The East End is not a conservative society, it welcomes eccentricity and odd impulses. It's capable of great hedonism and great seriousness. Working women are part of the fabric of life, so I found the daily mechanics of being a single mother there easier than in many other environments where it's a subject of endless speculation. Parts of the East End are still able to acknowledge the spirit of community in many conscious and unconscious ways—despite the appalling erosions that are being caused by redevelopment. There is a sense of living outside the mainstream of English life, with its vicious individualism and incomprehensible ambition, and a sense that individual survival is at best futile, at worst dangerous. There is the constant, warm acknowledgement of the need for society, for combination, for company; a dark and sure knowledge, which outside the East End I've known only in Ireland, that leads to the ties that bind being honoured.

Inside this context I did some of the best work I think I've ever done. *St Joan, The Hammers are Coming, George Davis is Innocent, OK*, and *Out for Nine* are all pieces that I'm still proud of. One of the reasons was that, feeling so outside the established framework of the theatre, my judgement was not impaired by notions of what others thought were 'names' or 'talent'. I was free to work with those people that I liked. Because of the professional isolation I referred to earlier, I am not sure how other directors go about their work, so I don't know how much to ascribe the way I work to being a woman. Once I am rehearsing I become totally obsessional: consequently I want to feel strongly about the people I'm working with. I'm happiest when I have what amounts to a loving relationship with a company, when there is a mutual respect of temperaments, views and talents. I hate discovering during a rehearsal period that I don't like an actor or that an actor doesn't like me, that we wouldn't cross the street to exchange views—because from that point on a certain inhibition sets in. There's a reluctance to venture into disagreeable areas, and the, at times, fairly violent push and pull, which is the essence of creating plays, is stilled. I loathe those rehearsal periods where I feel sufficiently disengaged from the actors to act the director, where, feeling that an open and direct relationship is impossible, one retreats into subterfuge and manipulation, knowing that there's no possibility of shared objectives.

I adore actors, and I don't mean that as a piece of theatrical hyperbole. As a species, their abilities and insights, when linked to a larger view ... which can be the play, the audience, an ideology, an idea. Acting is a privilege, and as soon as I sense that privilege is being abused by egotism and opportunism, I turn off totally. I try as much as possible to create companies of equal abilities, whatever the size of parts involved. There is nothing duller than watching actors of totally differing abilities struggle to create the same reality on stage. That is one of the many reasons why the work of the major companies is so lacking in any vibrancy and definition. Just as I have little patience with actors who see every play as a context in which to further their career, so I have little time for actors who are not very good at their job. It's such an arrogance to take over people's heads for two and a half hours and interpret reality for them: you've got to be fucking good at it. I know I can be very cruel when faced with incompetent actors, but it's always seemed to me too important to treat as a comforting hobby. I apply to my working life more or less the same range of sensibilities that I apply to every other aspect of my life; I see no dividing line between what I bring to both and what I expect from both. Most other jobs in the nation carry with them a necessary alienation. The theatre is one of the rare opportunities to become unequivocally involved.

The majority of actors at the Half Moon were all people whose judgements and taste I had a great deal of respect for. We developed close links with our audience and had a tremendous sense of the initiative being with us. If the press came and liked it, great. If they didn't, that had little effect on audiences who were not in the habit of reading theatre critics. It seems worth pausing over *George Davis is Innocent, OK*.

The campaign to free George Davis was, in terms of a working-class campaign against the status quo, one of the most original and potent of recent years. We felt we couldn't ignore it and proceeded to put together a show. One of the main areas of debate in rehearsal was how critical we could be of the campaign. We were sure that we'd fairly represented the extraordinary moral energy of its leaders, Rose Davis and Pete Chappell, but were critical of what we felt was their lack of analysis of the ramifications of the changes they were demanding in the legal system. We were, of course, nervous about being seen to impose our own ideas on a situation that we had not generated and were not a part of.

There was one leaflet that we gradually focused on. At the end of it there was a quote: '"We will fight and we will fight and we will win in the end." Queen Victoria to her troops in the Crimean War.' Shane Connaughton supplied a scene in which Pete Chappell (Alan Ford) and Rosy Davis (Mary Sheen) visit a Dockers' Union leader (Alan Devlin) to ask for support for the campaign. After supporting the campaign in principle, Alan had to begin to point out that it was a bit daft for a working-class campaign to be using as a rallying cry a quote from Queen Victoria and, more seriously, that the optimism and confidence of imperial Britain couldn't that easily be translated to a wholly working-class movement aiming itself at the heart of the British legal establishment. He then carried on to an analysis of how that establishment functioned.

The first night saw not only our local audience, members of the campaign, but also a fair deputation of East End

villains, all wholly suspicious of this decrepit synagogue mas-
querading as a theatre—not to mention a bunch of people
who could be earning a decent living on telly rather than
hanging about the East End. The first act went amazingly
well, but as we came towards the dock scene in the second act
I felt giddy. I put my head in my hands and thought, 'This is
it. This is where we lose all credibility and their scepticism
starts.' Alan said his piece; there was a deathly hush, as
painful to me as eating broken glass, and then cheers and
applause. Perhaps in a wider context those moments aren't
important, but at the time it seemed to me that a major trans-
action had taken place: we had established our right, not
only to record East End life, but also to add our assessment of
events to it.

I left the Half Moon for two reasons. Finding money to
keep the place going with a tiny grant from the Arts Council
was a daily battle—a constant borrowing from Peter to pay
Paul—to find enough money to keep the place warm and
clean and give people who worked there some kind of
minimum wage. I have an appalling temper, an anger that
can grow and feed upon itself until it is out of all proportion
to the initial abuse, and as I daily saw the struggle we had,
compared to the squandering of huge sums of public money
that the 'centres of excellence' indulged in, black moods
would settle in that I couldn't shake myself out of. The final
night of fury came when I went to see *Weapons of Happiness*
at the National Theatre. A Half Moon actor, Billy Colville,
was in it. There was all the usual National extravagance
evident as it proceeded to reveal a tale of working-class kids
in south London, so abstract and insulting my head ached
with anger.

I will not join that lobby that says the act of putting
working-class folk on to the stage of the National Theatre is
in itself radical. If one wants to write plays about the working
class one has also to face the problem of how to present them
to that class: the context is finally as critical as the play. One
would not expect the working class to sit relaxed over a cup

of tea discussing their problems in a Knightsbridge drawing room any more than one would expect a merchant banker to feel at home in a Canning Town tower block. But it sometimes feels as if those daft expectations lie behind the constant, usually inaccurate, representations of working life that turn up on the stages of our established theatres.

That evening I stood outside the National Theatre and howled with rage and the frustration of being English. But I had the classic female get-out clause: the man I'd lived with for a long time had returned to Canada and wanted me to join him there. I did.

I half hoped that away from England my obsessional appetite for working in the theatre would diminish, but without work I very soon became listless and apathetic, feeling at times like a prisoner of my own creation. The relationship collapsed rapidly and I found myself in a strange winter wonderland of a country, without enough money to get home and a son to support. The very foreignness of the country bemused and inhibited my usual set of responses. I had a skill; I'd do what I'd never have attempted in England and try my hand at becoming a perfectly conventional director of plays with one eye on the bank balance. It was, overall, an exhilarating experience.

Canada has none of the sets of signals that designate class in England, so I chose to ignore the more hidden signals that intimated the ways in which wealth and power were divided and to explore what it felt like to have purely artistic concerns. The first play I did was Trevor Griffiths's *Comedians*. It was the first time I'd worked with a large, all-male cast. I felt more than averagely nervous on the first morning, knowing that the situation was fraught with not only the potential of male–female aggravation, but also 'My God, she's a foreigner!' As it was, within the first couple of days we'd created a totally productive working situation. I found I really enjoyed not having other women around. I am sometimes made quite nervous by the kind of scrutinizing of sexual behaviour women can inflict on each other. The only other experience I've had of a similar working situation was with Nigel Williams's *WCPC*, where again I felt incredibly relaxed working with a great gang of fellers, feeling quite uninhibited about midly sexual impulses of warmth and recognition.

What role does sexuality play in the relationship created out of mutual perceptions, judgement, trust and dependence that is at the heart of a working relationship between an actor and a director? Certainly the people I feel I've directed well, whether male or female, have been those I've felt a great warmth towards and been excited by. In many ways it's easier to construct a relationship with a man, where sexuality can often be a short cut through the tortuous business of getting to know each other. My relationships with women have been more difficult. An actress I worked with in Canada told me that she felt strangely cheated, when working with a woman director, of the sexual warmth that happened when she worked with a man. But there are women whom I love and love working with. I guess I like those women I see as being similar to myself, who've gambled with their lives a bit, run the risks of male disapproval and possible loneliness in order to define themselves. Other woman often bemuse me, trapped as they seem to be within the twinned restrictions of vulnerability to male approval and an incredible dependence on it.

Possibly the most important play I did in Canada was Pam Gems's *Dusa Fish Stas and Vi*, a play inspired, if that's the right word, by Buzz Goodbody's suicide. I'd read the play before in England and felt badly affected by it. Pam charts so brilliantly the contradictions that can become impossible for a certain kind of woman to exist with. The play was important in Canada, in that it was being done at the big posh summer rep in Toronto, and was being regarded as the brave choice of the season. Women's theatre up until that point in Canada had had a very low profile and this was the play that could (and in fact did) open up that area of work.

I spent ages casting it, wanting to make sure that the

women had that confidence that comes from being well cast and that they were sympathetic to each other and the play. I thought it could be a fairly disturbing play to do and wanted a cast who knew what they were doing rather than suddenly discovering they were in the middle of an emotional maelstrom. They were fabulous, unearthing perfectly that balance between pain and resilient humour which is at the heart of the play. The women of Toronto practically stormed the theatre; we played to 103 per cent capacity, and the show had to be transferred.

I felt totally confused about it. On the one hand I was thrilled by the work we'd done on the play and the kind of responses it had got. On the other hand, I felt impossibly close to that nightmare inside. The thrust of the play is that it is impossible to be a thoroughly independent and able woman and sustain an equal relationship with a man. The more thoroughly decisive the one aspect of life becomes, so the bitterer one becomes at having no control or choice whatsoever over one's sexual existence. It's a truth and a reality that has to be explored but which I'm not sure I personally should not duck and dive. Fish/Buzz, the moral, intellectual centre of the play, begins to evolve a devious madness rather than confront the pain that the loss of her lover is causing her. The madness helps her to sustain herself and the other three women who've become dependent on her ability to deal with the world. She finally sits down and listens to something as apparently innocuous as Bob Dylan's 'Just like a Woman', feeling wholly cheated of such simple satisfactions while she can easily become the mistress of so much more complex ones.

I began to re-enact that line of thought over and over again, until I finally persuaded myself from it. Perhaps I am deeply crippled by being a woman. If that's so, then, as with any other hefty disability, I have almost to ignore it in order to function. Buzz was far more of a pioneer than I am in the conflicting demands she made on her life. I think her death left me terrified of making the same ones.

Pam Brighton

I did a production of Pam's *Queen Christina* in London in 1982. Again Pam deals with that deathly combination of power and impotence that can exist only for women. I think I did the play badly. I think I was too frightened of making that journey again. But whatever the private grief involved in working on Pam's plays, I glory in having had the chance to work on the plays of a writer whose pulse one can feel so intimately. My mother couldn't even fulfil her ambition of learning to type. Of course we're still struggling, but at least we have reached a point where we can make choices where we want to go rather than struggling blindly upwards. The immense progress women have made in the last twenty years is extraordinary.

Canada gave me lots of things I probably would have been nervous of accepting in England. I spent two summers in Stratford, Ontario, where Robin Phillips had created a company running at a level of intimacy and intensity that I felt at home in. I did Shakespeare; experienced the wonders of endless resources; worked with a wonderful designer who understood about harnessing them. But it gradually began to feel like the end of a holiday; reality began to beckon, however grim the siren might sound. I had to come back to England.

In many ways, writing at the end of 1982, England is grimmer now than I ever imagined it to be, a country trying to solve deepening problems with an increasingly limited imagination, a situation guaranteed to produce inertia and despair among its population. The established theatre seems to me to pander more than ever to the social malaise, a circus specializing in trivializing human experience and potential. Each production becoming even more clearly a watershed in the career of its director clinging on to the ladder to the top. I'm not sure women's theatre is the answer. *Pack of Women*, which I did shortly after coming back to England, taught me that when women have committed themselves to becoming objects of commerce and adulation they can behave just as badly as men in the same situation, perhaps worse, cloudy as the issues can become under the mystique of sisterhood. So perhaps it's my class that keeps me from pining for the whorehouse. When I read articles by women clamouring for representation inside the National and the RSC, I grimace. I have no intention of resuscitating those bastions of privilege. The future of the theatre lies, like the future of the country, in creating entirely fresh ways of examining ourselves and our potential for living together, of reviving and reconstituting whatever is left of our abilities to combine rather than compete.

Interpretations

MAGGIE STEED

Suddenly everyone is writing about us, and asking us questions about our lives, experiences, and attitudes, and generally taking great account of us. I think it is time to be very suspicious. Here, and in the United States, it is very fashionable to say you are a feminist. It must be, because even men are saying it. It'll be tragic if all the energy of the seventies becomes just another commodity, and we all help to create another set of stereotypes in theatre, television and film. You can see them being established already: the Victim. Suddenly Shakespeare seems to be full of them—weeping women ignored by the court. The Independent Woman. (You know, that film we went to see where we all argued it *was* a happy ending because she decided at the end that she *wasn't* going to stay with Alan Bates and the last shot of her was striding off into the sunset *alone*.) Capitalism and its agents, who are mostly men, is like an enormous vacuum cleaner: it just hoovers us up. It's been doing a lot of house cleaning lately. So we must be circumspect and clever.

My job is acting—when people will pay me to do it. When I first went to drama school I think I wanted to 'move' people. I remember going to see *The Nun's Story* when I was a kid and thinking, 'Oooh, I'm being really *moved* by this.' I also enjoyed the energy I was allowed to use on stage, and never got that feeling anywhere else in my life. I didn't know what 'moving' people implied, and my drama-school training did nothing to enlighten me. In fact it compounded the confusion. They taught us to walk and to speak, and we all tried to be 'good' actors. We learned 'style', that is, how to perform in Restoration plays, Expressionist plays, and Jacobean plays, and our teachers then decided how 'good' we were in relation to how near we came to that style. Strangely, we were never taught a Brechtian 'style'. I think that omission says it all really.

It was all in the tradition of Good British Theatre, and I'm sure many of us were very confused, and happy only in relation to the amount of praise we received. I know I was. The idea that we should get to know when and why certain writers wrote what they wrote, and the social conditions they were writing under or about, did not exist. Our judgements were never asked for. In fact we were warned against them. 'You are actors, instruments, it is your job to interpret a play, not to judge it.' The outside world, with all that was happening there, had no place in the curriculum.

It was all very reactionary and patriarchal, and a good way to train the passive 'interpreters' so needed by the theatre establishment. As women, we were already well trained. We worried about our looks. The pretty ones would get on. The others—of whom I was one—became well practised in playing Lady Bracknells. The few who had a working-class background played maids and, if they were lucky, Mistress Quickly. This was all in the early sixties, and we fell for it. I left at the age of 19, five foot nine, taller than most of the male students, with gappy teeth and the encouraging words from my principal that I was 'very talented but mustn't expect to work until I was thirty'.

After many auditions where I seemed to make it my business to dry so I'd know why I hadn't got the job, and a stint as an acting ASM, where I was constantly on the book so that the director could sit beside me and touch me up (I never said a word), I gave it all up. I went and became a secretary for five years, which is what all sensible girls do, isn't it? Obviously I hadn't made the grade. I didn't make the grade as a secretary either. I was kept in the back office with ladders in my stockings, whilst Sloane Rangers went upstairs and became producers' assistants, and I still didn't cotton on.

63

I just used to throw away the filing for revenge. Enough of tragedy.

I was typing throughout the late sixties and into the seventies. As with many women of a certain age, a lot of the things that were happening then began to influence me: Vietnam, miners' strikes, the women's movement. I gradually started to read and take part and not feel so lonely. It was like coming out of a shell. One New Year's Eve—I'm sorry if it sounds maudlin—I downed a bottle of gin and announced to jeering flatmates that I was going to make a comeback.

By the end of the year, I was working in theatre in education in Coventry. I wasn't inspired and clear in what I was doing, but I know that all those happenings rubbed off on me, just as they did on a lot of other people. And the work we did in Coventry was terrific. Anyone who works in a company that runs itself, tries to make theatre that is relevant to a chosen audience, and talks and entertains about the lives of that audience, is very lucky. They will have had an experience that will have made them tear their hair out but which also helps to make good theatre possible. A woman in that sort of set-up has the unusual opportunity to have a real influence over what goes on, and it is possible to gain a lot of confidence and clarity about feelings and ideas. So, as well as being culturally good work, it has to be good for the artist!

We did shows about old age, unemployment, pollution, that were theatrically imaginative, innovative and entertaining, and we did them for school kids from five to sixteen years old. The work of the Coventry team is well documented. It was a team with a stated Socialist perspective, high performing standards, and a constant fight on its hands to persuade the powers in education that its audiences wanted shows about the world they lived in and not *Tales of Flopsy Bunnies*. Our audiences were treated with respect, no matter what their age, and talked to as dignified, humorous individuals. Their response was dynamic. They laughed and they cried, and they were 'moved'. I realized that most of my training at drama school had been in order to give well-spoken versions of *Flopsy Bunnies* to audiences of all ages. No wonder we were confused.

For the past few years, I have been 'going straight' working in theatre and television. The more I do, the more I realize what Coventry taught me. There were other lessons too. I worked for the Belt and Braces company, who let me do Brecht's *The Mother*, when I was 30. My first big present. Shit, my principal had been right. A number of us, women that is, realized that we seemed to be playing a lot of men. We got frustrated. We had become quite good at playing men; we'd had a lot of practice, but it could never after all be more than an impersonation. We realized it was because the shows we were in were political shows, dealing with the capitalist world, the public world. And who runs it, this world? You've got it. A *lot* of mens' parts. Our lives, and the lives of 50 per cent of the population were not getting a sufficient airing, and it made us feel very uncomfortable, not to say angry.

These shows we were in were, indeed, correctly representing this world. You have only to look around you to see that it is true, and the women in the company repeated the process, many times, in serving the plays. They played silly secretaries, filled in the gaps when there weren't enough men, or got to play an evil woman when you really needed to show how horrible capitalism was. Suddenly things didn't seem as clear as they had. We were getting into murky waters, questioning stereotypes and symbolism that we had before accepted as sufficient to do the job and tell the story. There was a lot of blood. I think that we were lucky to have had that experience, because it was like an ABC of sexism. There was a number of women in the company who were all experiencing this *together*, and that fact has given each of us a lot of strength since then.

We weren't isolated actresses constantly going for interviews and subject to massive insecurities. Will he—the director is usually he—think I'm too old, too young, too pretty, too ugly, too passive, too frightening? What do I have to do to please him? At that time, we weren't on that market.

And if those insecurities sound self-obsessed and neurotic, that is what the experience of being on the market forces you into feeling, no matter how many days you start by saying it won't. If there were stereotypes working in Belt and Braces there are hundreds of them out there, in plays and films, art and sit. com. And even where the stereotypes don't exist in the material because of good writing, careless or cynical directing will expect them.

Enough of the treatise. What does all this make me feel now, and how does it affect what I do?

I try, as far as possible, to do only stuff that excites me with its potential. That's not an arbitrary ooh-what-a-lovely-part sort of thing, although that is important, but it's more to do with the spirit of the piece. I can only really give examples. For instance, I was in the television version of *The History Man*. I thought it was very witty and well observed as a piece of satirical writing, and I enjoyed thoroughly all the rehearsal period. The director took great time and pains with all the actors and the relationships between the characters, and all the actors gave their hearts to the playing of them. (I think, even with a character that you dislike, you have to find something within it that you can like, or anyway secretly admire, in order to open yourself up to playing it—there will always be a bit of you that is similar.) In the end, when it went out on the air, I regretted it, because it was in essence a very cynical and heartless piece of writing. A cold and unoptimistic story. That was a lesson for me, because I did enjoy the experience as an actress.

I don't think theatre changes the world. I think it does give information, uplift and *back-up* to assumptions and beliefs—right-wing and left-wing. Living when and where we do this support is predominantly given to the right wing, particularly on television, where the largest audience is. The right is sharp enough to realize this power—and we must be too.

It gives me a real thrill when I see plays and series or comedies that are well acted, entertaining and throwing *real* light on our lives, going into millions of people's homes.

I did another television series, called *Shine on Harvey Moon.* This was originally intended to fill the half-hour light-entertainment slot—an area to be wary of. Humour is always a laugh at the expense of something or someone; there's never much time for rehearsal; and there do still exist producers who become paranoid unless they can see four easy laughs on every page. *Mind Your Language*, for example, had many more laughs on the page than that, and every one of them was at the expense of supposedly stupid Asians, West Indians, Italians, etc., who couldn't speak English. The audience, predominantly born British and white, could sit at home watching this and laugh, comfortable in the knowledge that it wasn't about them. Off we go again, another set of stereotypes confirmed.

Shine on Harvey Moon was potentially a much better idea. The story was going to deal with an airman returning to Hackney after the Second World War. He was a good bloke, but he was also a bit of a loser. He'd played in the reserves for Clapton Orient in the thirties. He was expecting the brave new world that many soldiers were expecting after the war, and had to deal with all the things that had changed at home. These included a wife who had had a great time with the Yanks during the war and wanted nothing to do with him, kids who didn't know him any more, and no home (it had been blown up because his wife had left the gas on). So he has to go and live with his mum. This was not going to set the world on fire, but from the beginning it looked as though it was going to deal with ordinary people in real situations that can be very funny, painful and confusing.

On the page, the character of the wife looked very dodgy: the hard-faced bitch syndrome. Selfish, money-grabbing, embittered *and* a bad mother. But the situation left room to give the character all sorts of other angles which would explain why she initially appeared so unsympathetic. After all, life makes many people appear unsympathetic. It seemed worth a try.

67

Maggie Steed

We were lucky in that the cast and director all wanted basically the same thing from the series and the writers were approachable. We wanted to do a comedy series that didn't go for big laughs all the time, that allowed for subtlety. If there was a scene where the situation wasn't funny, we didn't want to feel obliged to find a laugh in it. Basically what that meant was that all the characters had the potential to be seen in a good and a bad light (as in real life) and that they could all have many sides to them. We all thought *Soap*, the American comedy series, was brilliant and during the making of the pilot talked a lot about how that series—now tragically cut because the Moral Majority got at the sponsors—managed to have the audience weeping one moment and screaming with laughter the next. *Harvey Moon* wasn't like that—it was much gentler and more sentimental—but we wanted to approach it in a similar way.

This agreement didn't mean that things were easy. I think they were particularly difficult for the women, although we did have some assets to play with. For a start the story really belongs to the man, to Harvey. The other characters are the world *he* inhabits. To change the emphasis or the way a situation developed in order to give either my character or my daughter's character more meat or another facet so that we weren't just serving his story meant demanding more space. (That meant either more time on the rehearsal floor, more camera time or occasionally throwing our 'hero' into a bad light in the audience's eyes. Or all three.) So, as things stood, I am afraid that the first thing we needed was a sympathetic leading man! Kenneth Cranham is a good, unparanoid actor who was willing to trust that what we were trying to do would serve the programme. So that was all right. Without that I suppose we would have been scuppered. Another asset was that most of the cast had worked in companies for a long time, so we quickly became like a theatre company ourselves, watching each other's scenes, making suggestions, changing things, encouraging each other. That doesn't often happen in television. It's more often a case of come in, do the crossword, do your bit, and go home. That particular dynamic is firstly in the hands of the director, who sets the pace, keeps things to himself, or decides how much participation is allowable. Some are very aware of guarding their position and others aren't. We were lucky: ours wasn't.

I'll give some examples of what we tried to do. A scene had been written between my daughter and my character that, on the page, looked as though Rita (me) was once again being heartless, fed up, and hadn't got a good word to say for anyone—in this instance, men. My daughter, whose function in the series seemed to be the goodie, the sensible one, who disapproved of her mother, was given some pretty prissy lines. We decided that, by playing the lines differently and by adding only a few more, we could completely change the emphasis of the scene, so that the two women could be seen as *complicit*: mother and daughter *amusing* each other about sex and men. In order to do this, we had to practise in the car on the way to work. This happened a lot. We did this in order to show a more polished piece of work on the rehearsal floor, which would then have more of a chance of being accepted. We should really have been paid from 9 a.m. not 10!

There was another scene, a post-bedroom scene, that had been written between Rita and a current boyfriend. This was a very crassly written piece, and could well have been that well-known number, the sex scene, négligé and all. We decided that we would both be fully dressed but looking a bit wrecked, drinking a cup of tea. (That's always a nice thing to do 'afterwards' isn't it?) We would play the lines with great affection and shyness, and make each other giggle.

There were many other examples throughout the series. We were also careful about what we wore, so that the 'glamorous' character (Rita) didn't always look glamorous, and my daughter didn't always wear twin sets. We also wore unexpected things. For instance, having decided not to wear the négligé in the love scene, later in the same episode, when Rita was very depressed, she wore just a petticoat. That wasn't cheesecake at all—most of us don't feel like getting dressed

69

properly when we're feeling down. It just looked a bit sad and vulnerable.

These may all seem like very small instances, but when most people are thinking about them all the time, and never going for the obvious solution, the difference it makes is enormous. On the other hand, whilst characters remain one-sided, whilst hard-faced harridans remain only hard-faced, whilst stupid Irishmen remain only stupid, they are not many-sided human beings and they do not *exist* in the real world. If they don't exist, then they can't take a part in it. You never see films about the Second World War featuring Indian soldiers, even though the largest conscript army fighting for Britain was Indian. No, it's always Richard Attenborough and Anthony Quayle going down with the ship. They are White, middle-class and male and so are allowed to suffer and be many sided. The world belongs to them. The experience with *Harvey Moon* taught us all a lot about stretching our minds, questioning our old assumptions and changing old symbols. There weren't many crosswords done. (I should also say that we did make mistakes as well, and there were a lot of problems that we didn't crack. There was one really interesting woman character who basically spent all of the series waiting to go to bed with Harvey, and we never really managed to do much more with her even though she was played well and interestingly. All her scenes were in relation to him, and the character was given no other people to interact with. If she had managed to come into our prefab, she might have stood more of a chance!)

That was a series that was being written week by week, although all the research and the basic plan had been worked out beforehand, so that the work we did on the characters influenced the writers, and as actors we were therefore pretty much part of that initial process. It is a very different thing from doing a play that is already written and completed before you get to it, particularly a classic which many people have seen before. Shakespeare's cast lists for the most part are very short on women, although there are also some beautiful women's parts to be played. It can be a very lonely job, being an actress in a Shakespeare play. One of the loneliest jobs I ever did was to play Gertrude in *Hamlet*. I was miserable and frustrated, and then realized that I was playing this part in this play, and all the other characters were ignoring her! She's only the lad's mother for god's sake! It is very difficult to paint a character's life on a stage if the writer hasn't written even a few clues, and it is also a problem because the temptation is to overpaint, bring your own frustration on to the stage with you and unbalance the play. (You remember the maid in a play when all she had to say was, 'Tea is served,' but she said it really angrily!) On the other hand, there are many productions of wonderful plays, by Ibsen, Chekhov, Shaw, Shakespeare, which I am sure completely obscure the writer's intention in the name of Art. A friend of mine went to see a production of *Uncle Vanya* the other day and when I asked her what she thought of it she said, 'Well, I don't know much about Chekhov, so I can't really say.' I had seen the same show and been bored out of my head: the only time I felt any recognition with the characters was when *they* were saying that they were bored too! I couldn't have told you what the play was about from that production. It had marvellous reviews. Under the titles of Chekhov's plays, he's written 'comedy'. He was a satirical writer and, for a lot of the time, his targets were privileged liberals at a time of enormous change in Russia. He was a bit of a class renegade. A good production would make absolute sense to many audiences of today. No one should come out of a theatre feeling so confused by what they've seen that they can say that. Angry, offended, uplifted, but not bored and confused because they 'don't know enough'. When Ibsen's *A Doll's House* was first produced in London they *changed* the ending so that Nora came back to her husband! *That* must have been confusing!

We have to be careful not to be intimidated by Art and by directors who are subscribing to it. They can be very frightening, and we, because we are employees and because we are women, do want to please. It is often very difficult if you have an idea about a character that seems to make complete sense from your own experiences as a woman, that seems logical and really quite ordinary—for example, that Gertrude is perhaps confused because of the way the world acts upon her—and it has no resonance for a director because it is quite simply outside his experience. Of course, it is his job to listen to your instinct and to reason with you, but very often it will not occur to him that questions should be asked about this person. (Whose story is this, after all? Very definitely not hers.) You can quickly be seen as a difficult and time-consuming actress. Tactics have to be learned. When to come on strong, when to let things go, when to smile and joke, and when to rehearse it in the car! I went to see Vanessa Redgrave in *The Lady from the Sea* and saw a play that was a heart-breaking story about the contradictions between a woman's secret life and what society forces on her, beautifully crafted, with the sub-plot echoing the same story in a more down-to-earth manner. Then I went home and read some literary criticism of it which said it was all about how good her husband was! It all goes to make me think we must have confidence in what many of these writers were writing, especially when they were trying to tell our story, because they've had the dirty done on *them* as well!

I would really like not to have to be aware of all this, not to have to become irritated and furious. I have to say that it does sometimes get in the way of creativity. There has to be a degree of safety during rehearsal in order for people to jump into the unknown and make fools of themselves in order to find the way to play the play. You do have to trust the censor in your head and give things the benefit of the doubt so that you are not constantly on the defensive. To have eyes in the back of your head and be constantly on the alert might be the best attitude on the barricades but not necessarily when rehearsing a play. You have to be brave enough to trust others, jump blind and throw all your ideas away.

In *An Actor Prepares* Stanislavsky talks about how we

should ponder on our character's hopes, intentions, class position, life history—all the material and spiritual things that go to make complex people. We *are* instruments, in that we make characters through choosing from our own experiences. Delving into our emotional memories and the knowledge and feeling that we are part of the half of the population that is ill-represented and ignored must play a part in that preparation, along with all the other experiences. Every woman we are asked to play will have suffered from that. Whether she is aware of it or not, that fact will have acted on her character, and we simply have to be aware of it and represent it somehow as part of her picture.

I want to finish with a word of warning about eccentricity. I think that if you are woman, and consciously reflect that fact in your work, then the results of your work at the moment will probably be perceived as eccentric. The dictionary definition of eccentric is 'not being placed centrally' and 'odd, whimsical person'. The first definition is pretty true, the second a value judgment! What can happen to you is that the powers who cast plays will start to think of you as an 'eccentric' person, with 'eccentric' ideas, and will not think of you for parts that they consider 'within the circle', the 'straight', 'serious' woman, the 'heroine', etc. These are the characters that remain in their world. You will probably not be thought of as Cordelia, Olivia, Nina, or Lady Macbeth. Of course, if you fit more into the current sexual turn-on mould—ooh, we're so bitter!—there may still be a chance, but it will be difficult for you. There are many actresses who, because of a combination of their looks and their attitude to their work, don't seem likely to get a look in. You see them only now and then, and everyone thinks they are wonderful, but a long time will pass before you see them again. I always remember watching Rosalie Crutchley on television. All her performances have been refreshing and uncompromising and believable. I *recognized* the people she played. I bet men thought she was eccentric. Now, of course, she is older, and so definitely 'out of the circle'.

We do have to take these parts for ourselves as well, otherwise we will all be playing Miss Prisms for ever. Miss Prism will do pretty well out of it, but Olivia will get a poor deal! I think this is happening a bit with me at the moment and I am definitely not the only one. It is difficult to glory in your eccentricity when it is stopping you getting work. It immediately makes you think, how can I be more acceptable? Should I have a nose job? Can I possibly look like Princess Di? After seeing me playing Rita on television, some directors are saying, 'No, she's too tough for this part.' Excuse me, that was in one character. Now, would they ever say something comparable about Ian Holm? We have all seen him be tough, funny, vulnerable—and in a multitude of parts. He is truly a brave and brilliant actor, but he has also had a lot of practice at it! He is multi-faceted, and so are we! When *we* present many facets, we are eccentric. So look out.

Up to now

CATHERINE HAYES

When I was five a new public library opened in Spellow Lane, Liverpool, around the corner from where I went to school. I joined it and filled my head with the likes of Nancy Drew, girl detective and Gary Halliday, airline pilot. Later, at Bootle library, when they let me into the adult section, I came across Graham Greene (he'd written so much you could hardly missd him), William Faulkner and many others, but the writer I really loved was James Baldwin. I used to think I'd like to be a novelist if only I had a story to tell. But, fortunately, after I'd been teaching four or five years and could foresee what the next few decades were likely to have in store, I realized that if James Baldwin had been brought up in Bootle, he wouldn't have had anything to say about the plight of Blacks in Harlem, so I wrote a novel about a friend of mine.

It was never published but I followed all the instructions in the *Writers' and Artists' Yearbook* and learned that one of the main problems for new writers is finding a publisher or an agent who will even consent to read your work. Some of the publishing firms I approached refused to read my novel (they didn't miss much actually) but I was still in the first flush of enthusiasm so I wasn't put off.

Then came my big stroke of luck. I read an article in the local paper saying that Alan Bleasdale, then resident writer at the Liverpool Playhouse, was inviting unknown writers to send him scripts with a view to producing a season of one-act plays. I was on my second novel at the time so I turned it into dialogue and sent it to him. After some rewriting it was one of five short pieces presented at the Playhouse Upstairs in November 1976 under the title of *Merseyside Miscellany*. Following that the Playhouse commissioned a full-length play, and then another one, and then I became their resident writer. One thing seemed to lead to another, but if it hadn't been for Alan Bleasdale and various other people at the Playhouse, or connected with it, I would probably still be trying to write novels.

My family had no previous connection with the theatre and although I'd seen quite a few shows in Liverpool and an Alan Ayckbourn and something starring Alec Guinness in the West End, going to the theatre didn't mean very much more to me than any other night out. I knew nothing at all about the workings of the theatre. If I'd thought about it at all, I would have presumed that the actors did everything except sell the tickets at the box office and the interval drinks. I had no idea what a director did and I hadn't a clue about how plays came to be written.

Perhaps that doesn't sound like a promising start, but in reality it was. I had no preconceptions, no idea what to expect: consequently everything was new and valuable. Very little disappointed me. I had no idea what could happen. I didn't know the career structure. I had no prejudices to get in the way. I just enjoyed it.

One of my first impressions was that the actors worked very hard. They put in long hours in poor conditions. It was often freezing. I didn't take my coat or scarf off during the first rehearsal I attended. It must have been warmer outside. I didn't know whether anyone expected me to speak, or give my opinion, or ask questions, or make the tea, or what, so basically I sat and watched and presumed they'd speak to me when they had something to say. Nowadays I do understand a lot more. I know what each person's job is and I'm more relaxed than I used to be, but my attitude is pretty similar. I love rehearsals. I think all writers should take part in them when they can. You learn so much and they're great fun— yes, I know there are crises from time to time. They're nice—

but I think the writer is more of an observer than anything else. By the time the play is in rehearsal your job should be more or less finished. It's lovely to see other people taking over and getting on with it. It's a matter of teamwork. Everybody has something to offer and your play improves as a consequence.

I don't think of myself as a writer. If anything I think of myself as a French teacher. Writing has never been my full-time job and I don't think I want it to be. Apart from the financial insecurity of not having a regular income I wouldn't enjoy the isolation of working by myself all the time. At the moment I find the solitariness of writing a good contrast to the exhibitionism of teaching, but it's too subjective to be my only occupation. Unlike in teaching where there are film-strips and tapes and course books to fall back on, and where you usually follow a timetable and a scheme of work, writing forces you back on your own resources and disciplines, your opinions, your beliefs; and the risk is that in feeding off yourself to this extent, your ideas and thought patterns become ingrained. You explore what's within rather than what's outside yourself, and that's a wrong emphasis. Really you need fresh blood all the time. New experiences. You need the world. Whether the world needs you or not is another matter.

I don't see any point in writing a play, or very much else, for its own sake. You have to have the strong possibility of a production to justify what you're doing and keep it from being self-indulgent. If you're not writing with a performance in mind, what's the point? There are other things easier to do and more pleasurable. Without a commission and a deadline all you're left with is a hobby.

What makes writing difficult are the limitations of your own imagination and ability. I've never connected those limitations with being a woman. I can't point to any example from my own experience that would suggest a woman writer is at a disadvantage compared with a man writer. I've felt neither helped nor hindered by being a woman. I object to the term 'woman writer'. I think it's as silly as calling someone a woman person.

As far as the limitations of my imagination and ability are concerned, all I'm sure of is that they exist. You've got to keep fighting against them, but at its simplest level I know there are certain things I can't do, like compose music or lyrics. So I could never hope to write a musical or a play-with-music. (In *Not Waving* the central character, a woman comedian, does sing several songs as part of her stage act, but these are songs I either knew already or came across in the course of the writing.)

I find the construction of a play difficult to manage. It's hard to manoeuvre a storyline out of my characters. Up to now I haven't written lightweight comedy or out-and-out farce and I could never imagine myself producing anything futuristic, or in the realms of science fiction. Although I like history very much I don't know whether I could successfully set a play in the past. I'm unlikely to write a political play. I'm not sufficiently interested in the subject, and it is in the pursuit of your own interests that, conversely, your limitations lie. And that's another reason for getting out of whichever room it is that you write in as often as you can.

I'm sure that to some extent men and women write about different things or at least emphasize different things, but I don't think that's of any importance. On the whole men writers have more men characters in their plays and women writers have more women characters. My writing will always be like that because I know more women than men and I probably understand them better.

I find it very difficult to work out the implications for the theatre of women's writing as opposed to men's writing. I think the division itself is artificial. You accept being a woman in the same way as you accept being British, or having dark hair, or many other things over which you've no substantial measure of control. It's not as if women are a new breed just invented. The struggle for women's rights took place in the past. I'm grateful that it did and that it was successful, but I'm not going to carry on fighting a battle that's already been won. Women are different from men, that's all.

What I do feel quite strongly is that personal information about a writer is usually unimportant and unnecessary. The writing itself should be the attraction not peripheral things like whether the writer is a man or a woman, or where he comes from, or how old he is, or what his family consists of. That might be interesting or it might not. Some people like to see parallels between what's been lived through and what's been written about, and, although it's obvious that the one does have a bearing on the other, they're not the same thing at all. When I was busy reading several novels a week it never occurred to me to wonder whether Graham Greene was alive or dead. Over the years I've picked up the information that Orwell, Huxley and Waugh are dead but Graham Greene isn't. I haven't been enlightened about many of the others.

My plays seem to me to be about ordinary people in everyday situations. They usually involve family relationships. *Skirmishes*, for instance, was about the problems of two sisters, the stresses, misunderstandings and antagonisms that existed between them, and how these were brought into focus by their handling of their mother's death. All of that is ordinary human experience. Very few people have smooth, tangle-free relationships with everyone they meet and we all have to face, at the very least, our own death, and, more often than not, the deaths of those close to us. That play could have taken place in almost any home in the country.

Not Waving is different, perhaps, in so far as the scene is a cabaret club and the main character a female comic, and female comics are still few and far between. But if her situation isn't as easy to identify with, her sense of isolation, self-doubt and rejection is universal. In the play these emotions are brought to the surface by the woman's illness, the break-up of her relationship with her manager and her failure to make club audiences laugh any more.

The plots of my plays are very simple. I'd like to be able to work out more intricate plots, but I seem to be better at characterization. My plays have so far been a mixture of sadness and laughter. I never think they're funny when I'm writing them but I love to hear an audience laugh at the lines. The language is quite simple. They're full of words like 'don't', 'won't', 'why', 'couldn't', 'wouldn't', 'I don't know'. The rhythm of the words is important. I read them over and over to make sure the rhythm's right. If you can't say a line easily there's usually something wrong with it. I pay very little attention to stage directions. I don't visualize my plays, I hear them, so it's of no importance to me what colour the walls are or whether the characters exit stage right or stage left. In fact I don't know which is stage right and which is stage left. When you're writing it's the words that do the work. That's why I find rehearsals so enjoyable. They put the flesh on the bones and make you realize what a vast difference there is between writing a play and putting on a production.

So far I've been very fortunate in that the directors I've worked with have been very willing to read early drafts of plays and make reasonably polite suggestions about what I should do with them. I feel very sorry for writers who have to work without the benefit of someone who'll tell them to rewrite. I think 'rewrite' is one of the most encouraging words you can hear.

What started me writing originally was a feeling of anger or frustration about certain things, notably the abortion law and its implications, beside which other contemporary moral issues pale. I felt and still do feel that I've got nothing in common with anyone who can talk about abortion without mental and emotional horror. I feel so strongly about it that I've long since passed the stage of even wanting to discuss the subject any more. I don't want to state my views and I don't want to hear other people state theirs because it does nothing but make me aware of an unbridgeable gulf between us. Sometimes I think that that gulf, in various guises, is what I'm writing about all the time, and it's got nothing to do with sexuality, or politics, or social class, or any other similar pre-occupation. It's more to do with the way people react to problems. It seems to me that problems exist on an individual level, but the solutions offered are more often than not designed to benefit the community, whatever that is, and alle-viate the community's conscience, if it can be said to have one. I'll never forget watching a television documentary years ago which opened with shots of child victims of the Vietnam War. The commentator asked whose fault it was that the children were in the state they were in. He then said pointedly to the camera and to the viewer in an excessively theatrical manner, 'It's your fault.' Well, it might have been the camera's. I don't know. It certainly wasn't mine.

As far as the future is concerned, I doubt if I'll ever be a prolific writer. I'm not bursting with ideas and I need to be pressured. I'd like to write, every so often, a play which is in some aspect noticeably different from my previous plays. The drawback is that there's no guarantee that you'll ever again write two consecutive words together, never mind something that'll amount to an evening's entertainment. But it's nice to try. I feel happier when I'm writing. I like the unpredictability of the whole business. I haven't found it glamorous but I have found it attractive and fulfilling. I want to continue to be associated with it.

Covering the ground

ANN JELLICOE

I was very lucky. I know now how lucky I was, because I knew what I wanted to do when I was four years old. I knew I wanted to go into theatre. Of course I thought I wanted to act. I still would like to act but now I think it's too late because I can't remember things, I wouldn't remember lines. I have a little dream that I'll go along to some amateur company and work with them, because I love acting.

I say the age of four because I was at this kindergarten as they were called then. They did a production of *Sleeping Beauty*, and I was Sleeping Beauty, and I had to say, 'May I try?' at the spinning-wheel. I remember this vividly, and after that I had no doubt, and always said theatre was what I wanted to do. There were moments later when I pretended I didn't, for semi-political reasons, but that's what I always wanted. I went right through school, not only doing as much acting as I could, but also making other people act. I was absolutely pestiferous—writing things, and organizing charades. I used to love charades. They were a very popular form of entertainment. It was during the war, at school, and there wasn't anything very much going on. Charades were a low-key form of theatre that didn't require any great hassle or have any great side to them. The interesting thing was I used to lie awake the night before we were going to rehearse them and work through every single thing. I would compose the whole thing in my head, and could remember it all, word for word, and would just teach people to do it the next day. Most astonishing thing. I couldn't do that now. I think my desire to act probably had something to do with the fact that my father left my mother when I was about eighteen months old and at that time my eyes began to cross. Clearly some tremendous strain was put on me. I have this theory that kids will go at the weakest point—with some it's stuttering. I was a bedwetter till I was about eight, and I was sent to boarding school—which was traumatic.

I went to the Central School of Speech and Drama—just did it in a perfectly normal kind of way. I'd written and directed essentially at school, and directed again at drama school. I didn't consider myself a writer—I didn't consider myself anything. I just liked theatre. The funny thing was, if any writing was required, I did it, without thinking about it. In my third year I won a lot of prizes at Central, so you could say things started for me around 1946–7. My first professional paid role was in French. A company came over from France to do *La Maison de Bernarda Alba*, and they didn't bring their bit parts with them. The word went round Central—who could speak French?—and I got a job with them. I did a short spell in rep, and then I was out of work.

It was just after the war, before television got going. There wasn't much work; it was a very bad time in theatre. There was no Royal Court, no RSC as we now know it; nobody was doing new plays. It was the recession before the flow. I was asked to be in what we would now call a little fringe group, a tiny company operating in the basement of an art gallery. They weren't very good. But I thought, well if she can do that, I can do that, so I started up the Cockpit Theatre Club. I wrote round to about eighty of my friends and said would they join for half a crown? They did, and we put on shows on an open stage. We used people who were in long runs in other theatres, and it was a Sunday club. That was the first open stage in London for about four hundred years, and we did some interesting things. I wrote my first—first to think about—play. It was a dreadful little play, and I also did translations of *The Frogs* and *Rosmersholm* for it. After that, my old drama school asked me back to teach—which meant to direct. I enjoyed it very much. I was doing about twelve Shakespeare plays a year. It was wonderful.

In 1956 the *Observer* Play Competition was announced. I felt, well, this may make you finish a full-length play. So I sat down and wrote *The Sport of My Mad Mother*. After that, it all just happened. It was very extraordinary, at the time, and to look back on. I had this little room I worked in, and then, when the results were announced, I was having lunch next day with Tony Richardson and George Devine. Then they were all coming round, and the model for the set was in my little room. It was crazy. I was buoyed up by these very loving people. George Devine was an angel in some ways. To be surrounded by this exciting atmosphere and then ... the bloody critics. Nothing could protect you from that. But even when the notices came out, it still went on, because the writers were very supportive. George had started the Writers' Group by then, so there were writers around like N. F. Simpson, Keith Johnstone, John Arden, Arnold Wesker—and some of the associate directors, like William Gaskill. All immensely supportive. I can remember being totally bruised—though it wasn't traumatic as the earlier experiences had been, perhaps because of that support. I can remember Keith, and Roger—who is now my husband (he's a photographer and had taken photos for the play)—and me walking down the King's Road Chelsea, eating a marzipan banana which we passed from hand to hand. But it was a good experience, in an awful kind of way.

Writing was then—it isn't now—often or always linked with emotional things, like unhappy love affairs. I've always written my best plays out of that. I had a love affair with Keith Johnstone which broke up. That was a desperate time and then *The Knack* came out of it. And *The Sport* was rather the same thing. Now, having gone through the menopause, and having really no sexual feeling left ... it's such a relief!

What I find with writing now is that I regard myself totally as a craftsperson. And I enjoy, I really enjoy, delivering the goods as skilfully as I possibly can. The community plays I do now—I reckon I write good ones, because I write what is required. I don't let my ego have too big a trip. I honestly don't think I'm capable of—at least I should be very surprised to see—another *Knack*. On the other hand, they're pretty good plays in their way. *The Sport* was written completely intuitively, sensing along, sensing whether a bit was too long. I still do 'sense' when writing—but that really was written with my eyes closed.

There were no conflicts over interpretation, because I was the director. This is what I mean about George Devine being wonderful. I hadn't any experience in the big wide world of theatre, but he obviously thought I was OK. He said that we'd do it together, protecting me against any of the other directors cutting up rough, but once he knew I could do it he let me get on with it. He'd come in to one rehearsal in four, and virtually never directed the actors. He was marvellous that way. I've directed all my own plays except one, *The Giveaway*, which was done by Richard Eyre because I was eight and a half months pregnant with Tom, and it wasn't on for me to do it. The best productions of my work have been done by me.

Sport was what Philip Locke called a 'flop *d'estime*', which was very accurate, and it was a quite painful experience. After that, I was still very much in the Royal Court orbit—I'd formed friendships and I went along to the Court a great deal. Then I suppose the affair with Keith began to grow up, and the old energy, the tremendous something having to come out. I decided I'd better write something that was going to be a success this time. There is that bloody thing, drummed into you at girls' boarding school, that it's not winning that matters, it's the joining in. The team is the thing. One now knows they don't want individuals; they want people who can be relied on in emergency to support everyone else. It's all for the British Empire. The Court had this thing about the right to fail, and I was in there with the old spirit of it doesn't matter whether you're a success or not, you just get on with it. I now know—bitter experience has taught me—it's terribly important to be a success. Otherwise you just don't get any more work. Lindsay Anderson learned this long ago. Anyway I thought I'd better write something that stood some chance. I don't know how *The Knack* came out like it did. A comedy with one set, four actors, about sex: it's absolutely cast iron.

Funnily enough, the Court had cold feet about it. George was saying, 'I don't know about this play, the first one was such a failure,' and John Osborne read it and said, 'You've got to do it.' I think it was due to him it got on. The Court started havering around, saying they would put it in their season at Cambridge then bring it to London for a week. I said, 'Oh no, you don't. If you do it for a week, you're labelling it a play you only have a week's faith in. Let it go to Cambridge and then take its chance—see if anybody else wants to buy it.' It was a wild success at Cambridge. You'd go up there, and all these undergraduates were queuing. It was bliss. If you didn't take up your free production seats the house manager was livid because he'd lost the money. It certainly wasn't 'Thank god you've come so there are two more in the house.' They were a lovely audience: they were so quick, they would see the point of a joke just before it was made. Oscar Lewenstein came to see it, and said, 'I'll take it in,' and when the Court heard this they nearly died. It was all very satisfactory!

I did really enjoy a lot of that experience. I can remember going out of the theatre just before the opening night of *The Sport*, and going Aaaa! Because they were just hoisting up the 'N' at the end of 'ANN', in lights. I went over to Peter Jones and had a cup of tea, and sat watching them do the whole thing. That was a very choice moment. There were awful moments after that. I heard on the grapevine they were going to take *Sport* off. I opened the paper one day, looked down the row of theatres, and it wasn't billed where it should have been. I rang George and he said, 'Come and have a drink.' He didn't want to, but he'd got to face up to it, so we went to the bar in the theatre. I got a gin and tonic in one of those large goblet affairs, and I was shaking so much I had to put the glass down or spill it. Then he actually dared to tell me they were taking the play off.

However *The Knack* was great fun. I think the best time was going out to dinner every night with Mike Nichols in New York. (He directed the New York production.) It was wonderful. I'd be wearing my old Marks and Spencer's clothes, looking like the wrath of god, but because I was with him those bloody people just rolled out the carpet. I remember Ken Tynan coming into Sardi's and standing by the table talking to me for half an hour because he desired to be seen with Mike Nichols.

There was not a great deal of money, but a reasonable amount, which I just blew—I blew it in New York. I didn't go over the other way, I'm too cautious for that, but it was lovely. I had a little apartment, and parties every night. All through life I've said, 'Am I enjoying myself? Yes, I am. Well make the most of it.' Or, 'Are you enjoying yourself? No, you're not, so don't think you were afterwards.'

By the time the film came, I'd had the fun, the success. I had very little to do with the film. I made very little money out of it. Basically £3,000, and a little dribble still. I feel so bitter about that: somebody must have made a lot of money out of it, and when I'm scrabbling about, trying to get our package fare to somewhere, I think, if only we had that money.

We really did feel we were into something very important then. Roger, who's a very innocent person in a funny way, was talking to someone at that time who said to him, 'I have the illusion of being on the periphery,' and he said, 'That's funny. I have the illusion of being at the centre.' That absolutely expressed how we felt for at least three years.

Between *Sport* and *The Knack* I wrote *The Rising Generation* for the Girl Guides. Someone in the Guides had heard I wrote interesting plays about teenagers. (They'd obviously never read *Sport*.) I said I thought teenagers were interested only in sex and jazz, and they said, 'Oh, that's fine.' But they didn't mean it. They meant write a worthy

87

play that has Mr Dogood and Mr Carry-On-Working and so on. They turned down my play because it was too tough. It's about the bomb. All the women get rid of the men, and the world is ruled by Mother—it's great fun. It was done at the Court as a Sunday Night by Jane Howell with about two hundred kids. It was probably the most successful first night I've ever had until these community plays. It was important because it did introduce me to the concept of an enormous cast in an arena—it was meant to be done at the Empire Pool, Wembley.

It didn't quite die, because sometime later I was approached by the county drama adviser for Hampshire to do a play. New law courts were being built at Winchester. (There was still a lot of money around at this time, though it was just on the hinge.) The Queen was going to come and open the law courts. They were all obviously hoping to get their knighthoods and their CBEs. They were getting the Queen there and they'd got to do something. They had the idea of a performance which would involve every possible resource from Hampshire. I was asked to do this thing, and I quoted a figure of £10,000. I was going to take £1,500 of that, which was a lot of money twenty years ago. They took it without a blink. I had a hilarious interview with the county clerk, or someone like that. I know these blokes now, but I didn't then, and I don't think I'd ever met anyone with more real power. They said, 'Where shall we have the dressing rooms? There's the barracks just behind—we'll move the army.' When I said , 'What about fire regulations?' it was 'Don't worry about that. We'll take care of it. And if you have trouble with any headmaster about rehearsals, just let us know.' It was wonderful. Within a very small area, they had total power. I began, but I didn't get very far before they decided to pull their horns in: they would not have the Queen; they would open the law courts quietly; they would not spend that money. So it never even got written, which was perhaps just as well, because I hadn't an idea in my head, and I was beginning to research into the history of the law.

Very quickly I would have come up against some very nasty problems, considering what that audience was going to be. So I was probably let off lightly.

I married Roger in 1962, and I had my family. I made a fairly conscious decision that I would spend time bringing the kids up. Though in point of fact I had a girl who came in every morning when I was supposed to be writing. I never did very much. I very slowly wrote *The Giveaway*—a slightly laboured piece of work but not without charm. It was a fantastic success in Edinburgh: it took more money than *The Prime of Miss Jean Brodie*.

I now say the best time in any production is when you're just talking about it to the managers. Everything is wonderful then. The difficulties start later. But honestly, then, with *The Knack* behind me, I was in the sort of situation where people would just beg. They would buy the play, then say very humbly to the owner (me), 'Do you think we could have a look at the script?' Sight unseen. Crazy. However *The Giveaway* was a terrible flop in London. Terrible. It was the only time I've ever been booed in the theatre. It was most unpleasant—but you live through that. There again, I was protected because Roger was so wonderful. Wonderful, unquestioning support. And of course I had a child a fortnight later so that gave me plenty to think about.

I'd forgotten all about *Shelley*. Bill Gaskill was taking over the Royal Court, and he wanted a play. And I wrote *Shelley*, which I still love. I don't think I directed it very well. I was a bit overawed by having people like Sebastian Shaw in the cast, and Ronald Pickup, who was very young, inexperienced, very good and not easy to handle. When I later did a production at RADA, I had a lovely group of students, and I rewrote ruthlessly—that was two years later and it was very much better. The other thing was that I was in awe of Shelley. I thought, you mustn't tamper with this extraordinary man. I remember having such a significant dream: trying to pack a suitcase, with far too much, not being able to get everything in, and the lid wouldn't close.

During that first season, I'd wanted to get pregnant, terribly, and I couldn't. Bill revived *The Knack*, but he didn't want me to direct it, or Keith Johnstone, who would have been another good person. He had the idea we'd have a fresh eye and he got in someone from outside. It was a dreadful production—*The Knack* is very easy to mistime. I sat in that theatre one night and thought, am I really going to spend the rest of my life suffering this sort of indignity and insult—and I got pregnant. Obviously I must have felt: pointless. Pointless.

When the kids were at school, five or thereabouts, and the household was pretty steady, Oscar Lewenstein asked me to be the literary manager at the Court. I enjoyed it a lot and stayed for about eighteen months. By then we had a cottage down here in Dorset and we came down every holiday, every half-term. I had the job at the Court on that agreement. It was a time when London was awful, around 1974. It was a time of riots and shortages and curious hysterias. I wanted to be out of town more and more. I did find a lot of women's plays while I was literary manager. It's not deliberate, it's just that you have a certain sympathy. I must have found at least three major women writers: Mary O'Malley, Felicity Brown, Lee Langley. I didn't 'find' Pam Gems but I asked her in after I'd seen *Ms Venus*, which I don't suppose a bloke would have done. You could always tell who was a 'Court writer', and various women who weren't headed toward other managements.

I didn't feel isolated as a woman in the earlier days at the Court. I was awfully blind—I'm one of the ones that's been re-educated. I felt I'd done something remarkable, being a woman who'd got through. And I liked that feeling. At the same time I didn't appreciate what tremendous disadvantages I was working under as a woman. I now think I was. The men didn't really take a woman seriously, as a director for instance. They weren't aware of it and I wasn't aware of it but I think it was hard. I think the dice were very loaded against women writers because all

Covering the ground

the critics were male and that made an immense difference.

Part of what I mean about realizing it's important to be successful—and this is very important for women—is the need to understand about building a career. I've now alerted my daughter to this problem. Once I was literary manager at the Court, I could have stepped on in all sorts of directions. I could have taken over the Theatre Upstairs, for instance. I think men map out where they want to go. They see a series of possible steps to get there. Supposing you want to run the National, you have got to be seen doing certain things, and you step-ladder your way up. I dare say women now are aware of this—yet there are never many women around. Here, the director of South West Arts is about to leave, and we had an Executive Committee meeting the other day. All these bloody men were saying, 'When the new man comes, he must have a free hand.' I said, 'Do you think we could say "the new person"?' We—the women—were talking about it afterwards, thinking what woman we could persuade to apply for the job. There are still not many women.

I think too that my way of working was incredibly feminine. By that I mean wandering round and searching out; sensing, not making lists and structures. Take Edward Bond: he's virtually got the whole play written in his head before he starts. I wander round the subject. And even now, talking to people, I much prefer to cover the ground in a hazy kind of way rather than have an agenda. I wasn't convinced that this was a bad way of working, or even an inferior way, but there's no doubt the fellers thought it was. I can remember having tremendous arguments with Keith John-stone, who was as far from a male chauvinist pig as you could get, but who wanted to convince me that a bit of music, to which he had a gut reaction, was right for *The Knack*, and I didn't think it was. Because I couldn't produce a rational argument he got very scathing. Men didn't trust you. They patronized you.

In point of fact if I had, for instance, run the Theatre Upstairs, I think it would have destroyed the family life. Back

91

to the old, old story. I really do think I felt, I can't do that to them. And I keep on thinking that. Then, recently, I met this seer, counsellor, clairvoyant. I can't explain what she does, but she finds out what you want to do, and she says, 'Why not?' She gives you permission to do it. She did exactly the same thing in a way with Roger. Until recently I'd been saying, 'I'll give this work up in nineteen-something—I'll do the next community play and then stop.' And I found myself saying to my friend, 'The only thing that would hold me back is my family.' And she said, 'Why?' Then she said, 'Your family needs you to be a success.' And I thought about this, and I realized she was right. I now realize what's happened. I'm passing out of a period when the children depended on me a great deal. I'm going into a stage in which I'm not needed by the family in quite the same way. All these things that are happening now are happening because the time is right. I was held back a lot before because I wanted to have children, then I was waiting to have them, then I had them. Now I'm pretty free of them and I'm going to be more free than I've ever been in my life before.

I did the first of the community plays after we had moved down here, in 1979. It started when I went to the comprehensive school up the road and said, 'Would you like me to write a play for you?' They said, 'Oh yes.' But the English master there who was responsible for the drama didn't want me encroaching, so when I took the play up, there was a sort of silence. They started saying, 'It's too big for us,' so I said—I was very proud—'I'll take it away in that case.' But then this bloke left, and I happened to look at the play one day, and thought, of course it should be done. So I got hold of the University of Exeter, who agreed to stage manage. Our local professionals, a community company, wanted to come in, and so did the amateurs from Lyme Regis.

I went back to the school, and rationalized it by saying, 'It's not too big for you because we're going to do this, and this, and that.' What we'd done, without realizing it, was to set up a community production. We had a very good woman who came down to do the design—and was paid absolute peanuts. Then a local woman who did the sewing for the local amateurs, wonderful woman, literally sat down beside the designer, Carmel, and they worked together. This woman said, 'Well now, we'll give these coats to so-and-so, she likes coats, and we'll give all those ruffs to so-and-so,'—and it was all round the town. The whole germ of the idea took off. The Town Council lent chairs, and the town banner, and the Mayor said, 'I'm glad to say, my dear, the vote was unanimous.'

That play, *The Reckoning*, was the first time I didn't feel a divided person. It was up there three minutes away; I was working in the town; I was working in the school my kids would later go to. I'd come home and be mum, Mrs Mayne, and I'd go out of the front gate and be Ann Jellicoe, playwright. From that moment I started answering the phone as Ann Jellicoe, because that's how people ringing me would know me.

The play was about the Monmouth Rebellion which took place here. It was extraordinary, the people of Lyme, in rehearsal and in performance, watching a play about themselves. There is a unique atmosphere. It's partly the promenade style of performance, partly that the play is specially written for the town, but it has never failed, that excitement, and they just go wild. After that, I was exhausted for a while, and then I realized I didn't want to do anything else.

I was an absolute innocent about the finances. Money's never been my strong point. On *The Reckoning*, I didn't get paid anything for the play, and I didn't even think about Arts Council grants. Carmel got £250 for the design. We got £790 from South West Arts (the Regional Arts Association). The play cost only about £2,000 to put on. Then, with that record behind us, I went to the Gulbenkian Foundation, and they gave us just under £10,000 for eighteen months, and that really got us going. The Carnegie Trust gave us £5,000 for capitalization—we haven't spent that yet, it's so nice to have

93

it. Then we got about £8,000 from South West Arts, and things began to get more comfortable. The biggest single step forward was getting funding for a part-time secretary, and we've just appointed an administrator, and I have an associate director who's working in Devon. We sat round a week ago saying, 'Isn't it great?'

We haven't deliberately set out to have all women, but we just like working together. There's a double thing about that—this may be unfair—but I say that 60 per cent of this work is social work; you have to relate to people. George Devine once said to me, 'If you knew how much shit I've had to eat to get what I wanted.' And this is precisely what happens here. You just eat shit to get what you want. I have a feeling women are more prepared to do that than men. They have more empathy.

The relationships that have to be set up, locally, are incredibly complicated. We go awfully slowly. It's virtually always happened the same way: somebody approaches you to come and do a play in their area. Every time is different. The fascinating thing is that they will say, 'Our town is marvellous,' or they will say, 'Oh it's a ghastly town, nothing ever happens here.' And they're absolutely right, whatever they say.

Then you very slowly set up an organizing committee, and talk to the mayor, talk to anybody you can find really. Then you commission a play—and that's a very dodgy business. I now feel I have to write an all-purpose back-up play that we can sling in at the last moment, and just put the local names in, in case a commissioned play doesn't materialize. Howard Barker, who wrote the play for Bridport, *The Poor Man's Friend*, was a friend of a local schoolmaster—and wrote I think his best play to date.

It is enormously slow, careful, detailed work. We hold workshops, and they are very useful. We really branched out in Sherborne, and did workshops with Mike Alfreds, Bill Gaskill, Keith Johnstone. They were amazing. They help to publicize the work; they get people in who would never normally have anything to do with the local amateurs; and they also get a discipline going, and an attitude to work.

There's an enormous amount on the agenda. Making costumes, the fair beforehand. I think we involve four times as many people off the scene as on. I'm never satisfied with the degree of involvement, I always feel it could be more. The largest number so far is about five hundred—a hundred and fifty, to a hundred and eighty in the show, and then loads more, some to a small degree. But I reckon if someone pushes a leaflet through a letterbox they feel involved.

It's such hard work, and it's so ungrateful to begin with. There are only a few souls who think it's going to work. It's total faith. You say, 'It will be all right. *This* will happen, and *that* will happen, and *they* will be for it, and *they* will be against it, and then in the second week it will take off.' And some people will close their eyes and believe you. I don't like auditions, but they do, because justice has been seen to be done. Everybody fills in a little form: name, address, telephone number, school, if any. You have a whole pile of papers for Monday to Friday: 4.30 to 5.30; 5.30 to 7.00; 7.00 to 9.30; Sundays. And you have a hundred and fifty people, each with an entirely individual life, saying, 'I have choir practice on Monday at four,' or, 'I have to take my kids to violin lessons on Friday at six.' It takes me a fortnight to organize a rehearsal schedule. It's just slog, except in rehearsal itself, which is perfectly normal.

The level of talent is amazing. I regard the cast as *actors*, not amateurs . They may not be not as easy as some of the most experienced professionals—it's wonderful the way professional actors can change, that flexibility they have—but they are marvellous. Take Jim Hoskins, who played Dr Roberts in *Poor Man's Friend*—he is a natural actor. But he's not unique.

I think what I love about it is slowly building something in the community, and struggling to bring the community in, in every way that you can. You get a sense of reality. You don't wonder who your audience are. Of course you hope to god they'll come, and they don't come just because of the large

95

cast; they come because the show is good. I love working with people whose lives you know about outside rehearsal. There's a sense of reality. It's not 'precious'. You know Jim Hoskins has his job; everybody in town knows him; you know what's going on.

It all started because somebody in Medium Fair, the community theatre company, said, 'Oh, you must have an interval, because then you involve people in making coffee.' And I suddenly realized that was what it was all about. If you got people to identify, they would want to understand the process. I'm trying to make theatre valued and respected—which it certainly is not at the moment—to make people understand the excitement of a work of art, why some people go so crazy about it. And I think the beginning is asking them to do something. Not just saying, 'It's wonderful, come along and watch it,' but saying, 'Help make it.'

Taking care of everything

I work at the Cockpit Theatre. It's an Inner London Education Authority building, so it's educational as well as being a theatre. I'm the technical stage manager. That involves overseeing all the stage management and technical aspects of all productions. I've worked at the Cockpit for about fourteen months, and I've done thirteen shows in that time. The turnover is pretty high. The standards have to remain the same regardless; you can't turn around and say, 'I can't do all this.'

I also run a Stage Management Course, and without that there would be no stage crew, so it's a necessary part of the job. I train young people between the ages of 16 and 24. They come in to do basic classes, and they have the option of working on a show. This year I've got nineteen in the group and eighteen of them are girls.

They go through the various aspects and processes. Getting together the props for a show is a big job that takes up a lot of time. We have facilities to make props, a large workshop and so on. They need to learn the running of a show—stage management jobs aside from the technical ones—being able to log the book, cue everyone who needs cueing: actors, lighting, sound. They have to be able to lay out a props table and organize props so that they're in the right place for the right person. We have a props person and assistant, who does the running round, setting out, checks on running props—that's anything that needs buying—every day. They learn how to make that go like clockwork. Taking care of the actors backstage is a big part of the work. The cast of a show can vary from fifteen to sixty-five, so one of our problems is noise and time has to be spent policing the cast who may be inexperienced. There's someone taking care of special effects; someone standing by to make sure there are no accidents, if you're using traps, and supervising anything risky backstage—explosives for instance.

Upstairs, in the control box, you'll generally have one lighting operator, follow-spot operators if necessary, and a sound operator. Then there's the stage manager who runs the whole show, takes care of the etiquette—calling the half, actors' calls—and makes sure all the checks before the show, on lighting sound and props, have been done by the half.

I stay backstage, to oversee and make sure that if any crisis arises—a sprained ankle, or somebody freaking out—it can be dealt with. You can't really teach people how to cope with those things. It comes from experience. You can begin to pass things on, practically, and not set up any mystique about it.

We do shows during the day as well as in the evening, so we have to strike at night, and then get set up again. Because they're inexperienced, they may be rather slow, especially to sus that something horrible has gone wrong, so it's agreed that for a 7.30 show the whole crew is called at 5.45. I organize the strikes, set-ups, timing and so on.

I deal with the designer, who also makes. I work in collaboration with her on shows. We have quite a schizophrenic relationship. We deal with each other as four people. She becomes the designer and technician; I become the stage manager and assistant. We've developed a way of saying difficult things to each other in the third person. If she has something to tell me, she can say, 'Oh, by the way, the designer said to me that this needs to be dealt with.' And I can say, 'Well, the stage manager isn't going to like it.' It's a way of working together in a fraught situation.

By the time I'm running the show for the performance period, she's already on the design for the next. I'm often in a situation where I'm waiting: if you're in stage management you can't really get on with props until the designer's got her concept worked out with the director and so on. Working with a designer over a long period, you have to find your own joint pace; whereas if you're working together on an *ad hoc* basis you tend to pace yourself to the way the designer works. Everybody's different. If I paced myself to the designer I'm working with now I'd be a dead woman. She's extremely speedy. I know sometimes she gets irritated because I appear to be much more laid back, but I think that has benefits. There's no point us just winding each other up. Sometimes it's extraordinarily touchy.

I have a block about making props. I avoid it wherever possible. I can hustle most things, out of anybody, for nothing, and I can find things, but I'm not a maker. I'm appreciative of things that are made, but I don't get any joy out of making them. Often I feel frustrated because I don't have the artistic wherewithal to carry things through, even though I can begin with an idea, and visualize how it will look in the end. If I approach the designer with a query at the wrong moment, obviously she may not have time to deal with it. Then I feel very defensive because I approached her for advice. One of the worst moments we worked through was one time when she turned round and told me I was lazy, which I bitterly resented. I tend to walk away from things like that. There are times when you confront things and times when you don't. Sometimes the moment it's happening isn't the most appropriate one.

Good moments are when I'm busily crafting away in the workshop. She likes that. A designer is quite dominant in that sort of situation—that's quite normal—though it can vary depending on the personality of the designer. Some won't let you touch anything.

I'm also responsible for maintenance, seeing the theatre is in good order. I work with the theatre electrician on the technical aspects of maintaining the theatre, in conjunction with the theatre manager. I do all the practical stuff, the technical back-up, but he takes care of the production money on shows. At the moment I'm in the process of negotiating a new sound system for the theatre. With sound I can do the basics, but nothing sophisticated, and with this system, which will cost in the region of £20,000, you've got to know what you're talking about. That's been interesting, having to learn, picking up that knowledge very quickly.

I think that speed is what I enjoy about practical knowledge. I've always worked in situations where I've had to pick things up quickly. It feels like knocking down a brick wall. If I feel I've got past another wall, or even taken out a small brick, I feel good. I enjoy going through the mental process of saying, 'This isn't difficult. Why are you finding it so?'

People often swap knowledge through jargon. That's something men are very good at. The jargon can be a cloak, a mystique that's not made available to you. I've had men in to talk to me about sound systems, and had to stop them and say, 'I'm not going to buy from you unless you can explain it. If you can't explain it to me, I can't explain it to a student, and somebody's got to learn on this.'

It's been quite an experience for me working on plays the majority of which I don't like. I can pick one up, read it through, think it's rubbish, and get on with it. I'd like to be more committed to the piece of work, but then I also value the ability to be objective, not completely carried away by the things you do. It amazes me that you can start with a completely ridiculous script and pull something together from nothing, something that works, visually and physically.

Of course, if anything's offensive to me as a woman I'll have to say something. If I feel like that, then a lot of people coming into the theatre might as well. Though you don't always get listened to. With some directors, you can say, 'Why's that line in? Why do they say that?' And they'll discuss it with you; others you'll just have to put up with it. I think that's appalling. If you're a technician in the theatre you tend not to be seen to be creative, or to have an opinion on the thing you're working on. You're seen to be very much in a servicing role.

Directors puzzle me. I think it's the loneliest job in the

world; it has no appeal for me at all. Your attitude varies according to what the director is going through; sometimes it's impossible to pick up on that; they get locked in this thing of being alone. You can pick up on the desperation of that, even if it's hard to respond to it. Some directors will protect the actors and give you shit; some will tell you what idiots they think the actors are and always treat you well. It's very random, that relationship. We had a terrible situation with a director on a show with a cast of sixty and a stage crew of twelve. He used to wrap the actors in cotton wool, and then come back and give the stage crew a hard time. If you put your anger where it doesn't belong, it creates a split. It's very divisive.

Once, I'd sat in on a warm-up, and the director had been as sweet as pie to the actors about all the cues they'd missed. Then he came backstage and laid into the crew. What the director says goes, and I do adhere to that. The arguments you have in private are not the same as those you have in public. He was demanding an apology when he had no right to and I was silent. The kids in the crew were all looking at me. There are times when you have to go through this, and then go on with it outside. After the director had gone, I said, 'You don't have to apologize. You don't have to say you're sorry. You can say that it won't happen again. That's quite different. You've maintained your self-respect. You never need to grovel. If somebody wants to be a pig, they'll be a pig. Don't take it on.'

My job is to keep the situation smooth. The director's primary responsibility, to the actors in rehearsal, has to be supported. There should be an easy way of telling a director no, because it always upsets them. A director will try things on. That's what they're there for. They will behave extraordinarily—chuck things, whatever. You want to go away and giggle to yourself, but in that situation you must remain as straight as possible. If you get a director who treats you like an idiot that's always insulting. Generally speaking, if I say no about something I mean it. But basically the job's about supporting the director. Though there are some I wouldn't want to work with again.

Lighting is something I miss. At the moment it's not possible because of all the other organizing that I have to do. When I'm the only technical person responsible for overseeing a fit-up, I can't concentrate solely on lighting design.

I went off to assist on rigging during a fit-up at the Lyric Theatre recently. We worked all night. I really enjoyed it. When I started I was lucky enough to work with a man, Whitsun, who didn't object to passing on his knowledge—he was my mentor. He worked with practice, not theory. He'd give you something you didn't know how to do, say he'd come back for it later, and expect you to sit there and work it out till you got it right: like putting a lantern back together again, which is daunting if you've never done it. He never made me feel that I couldn't, or wouldn't, do it. If you challenge a child and tell them they *must* do something, they'll come down to 'can't' or 'won't'. You create a mental block. He didn't do that. Working with him, and learning from him, I was never talked down to or made to feel idiotic about something I'd asked. Sometimes he might tut-tut and say, 'Don't you remember?' But that was all.

After that I moved into a situation where I had to produce this new knowledge and I was challenged many times. It came, in two ways, from men in lighting in theatres I'd been touring to. Either it was, 'I'm not going to let you do this. I don't think you can.' That demoralizes you, and stops you working and gaining any credence in yourself. Or it was, 'If you say you can do it, do it, and do it better than me, and you won't get any help, even though I would.' That challenges you, but it's not a right challenge.

It's frustrating when you come across someone you'd like more knowledge from, but they cut you off instead. I could never admit to making a mistake, or failing. I had to work it out. That's good in some ways. You learn to work on the tips of your toes. But it can mean you're skimming, when you haven't the chance to really learn, for your knowledge to grow and deepen. In practical work, you do learn from other people. To be able to ask someone why they did something that way, and not be patronized, is wonderful. But you're asked into power games all the time, to prove yourself, to be better than, show how much you know.

Some years ago I was touring a show. I was taken across to the chief electrician, the lighting designer, by the stage manager. The chief was a big guy with tattoos up his arms. The image I have of myself and what other people have of me is quite different—when I'm working in that situation I'm actually larger and darker and stronger. I'm five foot nine and brunette, not lightweight and small and blonde, and I can't be patted on the head and treated like a little girl. I walked in and the stage manager said, 'This is the company's technician.' He looked me up and down and said, 'Really?' I knew I'd taken it on, in that one word, that I had to take it on. I was either going to get my job done that morning, lighting the show, or I wasn't. He gave me the runaround, all morning. In that sort of situation you have to work much harder and keep your wits about you. If you ask for something, you've got to make sure you get a reply. I'd say, 'We haven't focused that yet,' and he'd turn round and say to no one in particular, 'She says we haven't focused that yet.' People talk like that ordinarily in the work, but you know when it's about something else. He had five guys working for him, and his deputy, who was also running the show, said, 'Don't ever apply for a job here. He wouldn't employ you because you're a woman.' I must've got up his nose, because he had to deal with me, and he didn't want to.

That morning we went on, got it rigged and focused, and then we had to get it plotted. They got the tables out; the operator went to the box; the chief electrician sat beside me with his deputy on the other side and the other two guys behind me. He said; 'There you are. Do it.' At this point I was on the boil, I'd been working all morning with this bastard. I thought, 'OK, you want to see me work. Now I'll show you how.' I plotted at speed, as quickly as I could, running through setting up every cue and all of that. There is a choice. You either cop out altogether in that situation or you run with it. So you run with it.

We got on with playing the show, and he kept popping in. You pick up on that; you start getting worried—because there is that sexual challenge as well and it can't be ignored. I've often thought that I'd like to have a drink with a guy I'm working with, but that he'd think it was a come-on. So you go off home instead. At the end of the week we had some wine in the theatre and as we were leaving, he said; 'You know, I'm a real bastard to work for.' I said, 'Yes, I can imagine.' He said, 'I'd like to see you last here, the kind of work we do, so maybe if you're ever free, give me a call.' I said, 'No, I wouldn't work for you. I don't like you.' That showed him I hadn't gone out to impress him. It's my job. I expect to do it well. I took my anger away with me.

Lighting isn't a completely practical process—the end result is creative. You can colour it, move it, shape it. It's fluid: the variations are infinite. Mixing, matching, shaping—you could go on for ever. The enjoyable thing for me is that I've got to tackle these very practical things to get the effects I want. Two lighting designers together will argue endlessly about why they've used what, and the way they've used it, talking in essentially practical terms about this art. I like colour a lot, but some designers will spend years trying to develop for themselves a perfect open white even light that exists only on stage. I tell students all the time to go to art galleries, to look not so much at the paintings as at the light, where it's coming from. You can get all sorts of inspirations from light—whatever room you walk into it's always different, what it does to people is different. I'd hate to just hand over the design though, because when you're doing it practically, something very pertinent can occur to you —you can solve your problem by moving something a foot.

There are certain problems in plays that you can solve with lighting that you can't solve any other way, by using anything else. Lighting can be the star too. I've never quite got over the fact—I think it's indicative of the job I do—that there's something about that time when you've done the fit-up, and none of the actors is there, that's very special. You've got the lighting, a state up on a set that works well, all the bits and pieces, the set dressing there. It's very peaceful, that moment when you're all done. The job you do is putting everything together for the actors to use, yet there's something about the human form when it moves about that I find quite disturbing. You move light, and it's a great deal more fluid—less irksome, and erring, than this human form and voice.

The number of actors who can walk into the theatre and not see anything amazes me. 'Oh, that's the set is it?' You have to make that not matter to you. You could've been up for twenty-four hours, and someone trips in and says, 'Where's the dressing-room?' You are obliged to gratify the actor, unless you're going to be seen as very rude. It doesn't happen the other way round. I think that's where the coolness between technicians and actors sometimes arises. It's a pity.

All actors should have an experience of working back-stage, and technicians should know what it's like to go out there. I can't stand it when people call an actor temperamental. It means they don't know what that person's going through. If you stand in the wings with an actor and don't pick up on nerves you've got to be pretty insensitive. You can't help, and that's what you're there for. It's all aiding and abetting what goes out front. Your satisfaction comes from doing that part of the work. If you have to have applause as well, you shouldn't be backstage.

Liking acting is primarily what led me into theatre. I had a very good drama teacher at school. I fell in love with her and thought she was the most wonderful thing since three-coloured ice-cream. I went to drama school thinking of myself as a performer not a technician. The reason I stopped very early on was that I felt marionette-ish. I wanted to be outside and see what I was doing, and I couldn't and I found that frustrating.

I think there's a very definite personality that goes into a performer, quite split, to do with being childlike and vulnerable, and also to do with being a hustler. How do you balance those things and survive? I wanted to see what was happening, and add to it, and that's what I embarked on. I would never perform; I've no desire to; it doesn't appeal to me at all. I've great sympathy for actors. I don't understand them; I think they're crazy a lot of the time, but I still find it a thrill to see a play I think is well done, but I always want to work on it, not be in it.

Some of the younger women coming up don't recognize there is any problem, and just breeze through. But you have to go through personal blocks with some of them. There was a girl in the summer, operating lighting; she'd never done it before. It was a big jump for her to take. She had hysterics in the box. I sent the lighting designer up, but second sense told me I should go up to her. He was standing watching her. He went, and I asked her, 'What is it?' She said, 'I can't do this. I'm hopeless, useless. I'm a terrible person.' That's what it comes back to, that personalizing: I'm awful, bad, all the negative things. I told her that there wasn't any way out, that there was no one else, that she would have to do it. I said, 'You've got to get all the bits of you that are lying on the floor and put them back together, close off the rest of it, put the blinkers on, and just go for it. Make a mistake, fuck it, forget it and move on. That's what achievement's about.'

She turned round and said, 'Do you think I can do it?' I've thought that so many times, wanted to, needed to, ask it. I said, 'I'm going to leave you alone here for five minutes. Then, when you're ready, buzz down to me, speak to me and let me know you're ready to go.' Which she did, and we got through. It was touch and go—she burst into tears quite a lot after that. She had the kind of personality that wanted to get it right, and was frustrated. You've got to walk before you can run. And I was desperate for her to do it. I really didn't want her not to do it. You do sometimes have that painful thing of saying to someone, 'There's no way out. I'll be here. I'm here. I'm not unsupportive of you. I'm not making fun of you, but you've got to go through it.' And that's difficult.

Insider

LIANE AUKIN

Looking at television this year (1982) I was overwhelmed by male visibility. Men at war, in the Lebanon, in the Falklands; men unemployed, in dole queues, and picket lines; men at play, football, cricket, rugby, darts, snooker; men praying, priests and Pope. The action is always male, the centre of every event, male. Men are reporting on these events, men comment on them, men discuss Mankind. Men are the groups, the packs, the teams. Women are the 'others'. It is Man's world and women are trying to make the occasional appearance. Channel 4, by contrast to other television networks, is employing an unusually large number of women. The press—all of us—are impressed and thrilled to be able to point this out. Mrs Thatcher, our first female Prime Minister, is known as 'the Iron Lady'; Ted Heath was known as 'the Grocer'. The impact of the Greenham Common Peace Camp is based on it being exclusively women. It is successful and powerful, and consequently phenomenal. Anything successful and all-women is still thought of as 'phenomenal'. Women, as was always the case, are intricately involved in the economic and social life of this country, but their visibility is still always placed in parenthesis; it is special, it is unusual, it is minimal. Our perception of women is ordered in this way. Who has been responsible for this ordering?

Every woman is condemned to the experience of being isolated, of being a lone female in a male world. As a member of the female sex she has been classified by the dominant male world. These classifications are too well known to bear repetition, but they are all based on her physical appearance, her bodily functions. We know that this perception bears only a minimal resemblance to our sense of self, but we have been observed for so long that we are more concerned about what we look like than with what we are. Self-consciousness, as opposed to self-awareness, is neither a happy nor a healthy condition for people involved with making creative truthful statements about experience. So women have formed alliances with each other, accepted that they belong to a class/group, and they want to redefine themselves in accordance with shared personal experience. The object of this action is twofold. Firstly we want to be in a position to interpret and question *human* experience instead of leaving that to one half of the species, and secondly we want to gain a more realistic and complete sense of our *individual* selves.

Few professions can have a higher visibility factor than acting. An actress is the physical embodiment of someone's idea of some woman. She is standing there for all to see. As a young actress I was told that I couldn't play young girls. I was too tall, my voice too deep, my features too pronounced. I'd been to see plenty of plays, so I knew they were right. But—they said—your day will come. By the time I was old enough to play the parts I looked like, my day had come, but I had gone. It happened this way.

I was rehearsing *The Homecoming* by Harold Pinter and playing the part of Ruth. Ruth is a mysterious, ambiguous and not fully realized character. She is the only woman in the play. The play is set in a household of men. One day one actor came over to me and asked me whether, during one of his speeches in a scene we played together, I would sit on the sofa, cross my legs and swing them very slowly. A day or so later another of the cast talked about the scene we had together. Could I try and pout more, he asked, and maybe stick out my boobs as well. It would help a lot, he said. A few days later, the director suggested I think of Ruth as an 'earth mother', and he asked me to try and embody that feeling more fully. At this point I got my act together and had a blinding insight. They had all been asking me to act out their fantasies about female sexuality. I told him that it didn't matter whether I swung my legs or not, whether I pouted and had big or little breasts, whether I came on looking like Jeanne Moreau, Gracie Fields or the back of a bus, there was only one thing I had to do, and I didn't feel there was any problem about not being able to pull it off, and that was—be a woman. Ruth is a catalyst in the play. She is the female presence in a world of men. Just leave me alone, I said, and if there's still a problem, it isn't mine. The production worked remarkably well.

I can't say that Ruth was one of the most interesting parts I have played but it was a turning point in my feelings about myself and about being an actress. I had had to confront the problem of being a woman and yet being asked to play a woman. After twelve long years I had managed to identify a male projection of woman as a sexually defined person and I decided it was time to find my 'character'. I decided to stop acting and turn more to writing and directing. I wanted more control over my life and my work. I didn't need to play a part in order to 'be' someone. I, like so many other women, had decided to COME OUT.

An aside about why I decided to stop acting: my marriage had ended and I was bringing up two small children on my own. I felt I couldn't accept work that meant me leaving home for long periods. There wasn't enough work about to ensure I could earn what I needed. To be a performer you must be a hundred per cent 'there' physically and mentally. Given my domestic situation, it was rare that I felt *sixty* per cent 'there' at any time, let alone at curtain up. It's not easy to play Hedda Gabler and Mother at the same time.

During the following three or four years I wrote a lot, did some directing, taught, and spent a lot of time involved with the women's movement. Sometimes this overlapped with work, sometimes not. I was involved with the Women's Theatre Seasons at the Almost-Free Theatre and the Haymarket, Leicester. They were both exciting and important projects but the centre of my emotional life was the learning experience of being with and talking to women from all walks of life and taking part in various actions which developed theory out of practice. I was still an outsider, one of the 'others', but I'd been reclassified as Liberated. I was still overworked and underpaid, I still felt unease and a great flow of anger, but this was no longer considered a personal idiosyncrasy. It was given official, political status. In 1975 I was asked if I would like to join the Drama Department of BBC Radio Drama. I was nervous about giving up my freelance status but excited at the opportunity to be able to exert editorial influence. This was the sort of job that we women were demanding to be given. I accepted.

An aside about why I went to the BBC: I love radio. I wanted to earn a regular salary. I liked the idea of having a small power-base, a chance to learn skills and use first-class facilities. I wanted to direct. More than anything else, the idea of going out to work regularly and rearranging my domestic chores was an opportunity not to be missed. Legitimized freedoms!

During my first six months at Broadcasting House my mind was blasted, my identity in crisis. I smiled a lot, refused to make my office in any way 'homely', wouldn't have photographs of my children on my desk, often had my children sitting on my desk, insisted on going home at four whenever it wasn't necessary to be in studio, threatened to stand a dustbin outside the office door, thought of hanging a washing-line between mine and the next office (occupied by a woman), discovered that my male equivalent was earning several hundred pounds more than I did—because he had a wife and children to support?—rectified this, read nearly two thousand scripts and felt like the only girl at a boys' school. I also felt privilege. I might be a woman but I had passed for a man . . . or so I felt.

My first radio production was a play called *Delivery* by Valerie Windsor. It is about childbirth, an account of the experience of labour. The play was extremely successful, it had a particularly large audience and received a spectacularly large mail. My last production for the BBC was *War Music*, an account of Books 16–19 of *The Iliad*, by Christopher Logue. *The Iliad*, one of the corner-stones of male culture, is an epic about war, male homosexual love and masculine heroism.

Between those two productions I worked on somewhere around one hundred plays, features and readings. A large amount of my work was written by women. It also included work by 'ethnic' writers and this was gradually extended to include work by Third-World authors. I would conclude from this two things: one, the idea that women's writing is not confined to domestic situations gained credibility; two, the words 'woman' and 'radical' can become synonymous.

When I received the manuscript of *War Music* I was aware of the contradictions it posed. Many women would be critical if I involved myself with such material; on the other hand I was very excited by it. I think the writing is superb and I considered that to work on a production would be a great challenge, not because of its ideological content, but because it was so good and so demanding. Homer and Logue are recounting an exclusively male experience. As a woman I was excited at the possibility of exploring this experience. If I refused it would be only on the grounds of being female.

I was sure that the time had arrived when I must trust my instinct (backed by professional experience and a more developed consciousness) to act as an individual and not be afraid of betraying myself or other women. Working on *War Music* was both exhilarating and liberating. The production had three transmissions in six months and a very good press. Whether anyone would know it had been directed by a male or female I have no idea. Is the choice to use strings, flute and piano rather than trumpets and kettledrums a female choice? Was the choice of pace, silences, overall concept, female? They were my choices.

If I still have a lurking feeling that I have to justify this particular piece of work, then it's worth adding that a woman director may feel politically more justified in doing a production of *A Doll's House* or *Miss Julie*, but I would suggest that she is more compromised in attempting to rationalize Ibsen's or Strindberg's realization of a major female character than by dealing with an imaginative rendering of primary male preoccupations. It's an endless debate.

War Music, together with *Delivery, Animals in the Zoo* and *The Mouse's Tail*, both by Gaie Houston, and *The Dybbuk* by Paul Anski are productions I look back on with great satisfaction. When I joined the Department, out of thirty editors/producers, five were women. Of those five, I was the only one who had been married or who had children. Today, seven years later, the ratio of women to men has dropped slightly and some recent statistics show that the number of plays by women being transmitted has dropped accordingly.

At Departmental Meetings there might be a discussion about whether women's voices change after menopause. No one asked my opinion. When actors wrote asking for work, they were discussed in terms of their work. When actresses wrote, their photographs were held up for all to see. (Why did they send their pictures? I suppose they know the rules.) Eventually, I became aware of my four female colleagues and slowly we reached a sort of unstated understanding that we must support one another because we shared a feeling of 'otherness', a feeling of difference which we never articulated. This understanding affected our public behaviour. When one of us spoke to a principle or a play, the others gave their support. Just knowing that other women were present, even if they were silent, was enough to ensure that a woman did speak. Without that collective presence I think it's doubtful whether I would have had the courage or confidence to say some of the things I said, to pursue some of the objectives I pursued. Men are more inclined to respect a collective presence: an individual cannot then so easily be dismissed as a 'crank', as having 'a bee in her bonnet', as being 'hysterical', 'paranoid'. I am convinced that whatever

113

one woman achieved in her work and advancement was due to the fact that other women were there and that had she been alone she would have had a different history and suffered more from her isolation.

Creative work is not the result of individual effort. It is the product of an entire environment. There is a pool of ideas and preoccupations to which many people have access but the creative artist also needs support systems both materially—which means opportunity of time and space—and psychologically—which means being encouraged and given confidence. This support can come from personal relationships: family, colleagues, friends. The gift of the new women's movement of the seventies and the eighties, in my experience, was the generosity and support offered by other women and the pleasure I had from responding to that support, offering it back in return. Today there is a network, a team, and the proliferation of women writers bears testimony to this. It is not that one *ex*cludes men but *in*cludes women.

Another thing I learned while working at the BBC was how easily one sees what one is told one can see. I had this sense of women being a minority but then one day I noticed that I was, in fact, surrounded by women. They outnumber men by two to one. Many of the technical staff, clerical workers, administrators, are women but because they are not directly involved with the 'creative' process and therefore have lower status, their presence is almost unfelt. Many of these women came to the meetings and even though I did see my four female peers, I failed to notice the other ten or so women present. Because the men behaved as though they were not there, I behaved in the same way. I was seeing the world through their eyes. I saw a room full of men. After five years of consciousness raising, I still fell a victim to this powerful perception and I was shocked to realize it. When I did, things began to change.

Increasingly interesting, as time went on, was the process of how work is done. Content you can control, process is a greater struggle. I sometimes wonder if a woman were Managing Director, Radio, whether the system would change, but I suppose it's like wondering whether, if a woman were C-in-C of Nato, there'd be no more wars. Large organizations and institutions, with all their vices and many virtues, are implacable, and no individual can make radical changes. Both men and women, whether they like it or not, are subject to the strength of a powerful and deeply rooted structure like that. How much of myself was I beginning to censor out by being continuously exposed to a dominant, if elusive, ideology? After all, I had successfully censored out those faces. The eye elects to see not what is there but what is powerful and persuasive.

I tried, for a long time, to get the Department to consider the possibility of job sharing, six months on, six off. This, for me, would have been a perfect solution, but the administrative difficulties were too great. Two years ago, I left.

An aside about why I left the BBC: I wanted more time to think, more time to concentrate on my writing. I wanted to work in the theatre again. I'm temperamentally uneasy about accepting a pre-planned life. As my children grew up I'd be able to test what I want to do against what I have to do, and sitting at my desk in Broadcasting House I began to wonder if the price I was paying for some kind of success was an emotional hysterectomy. There was a hell of a lot of love and hate that I was becoming expert at repressing. I'm not worried about being thought inconsistent. Every experience is a coherent part of my life.

Drama is a powerful medium for the transmision of ideas, and theatre particularly so. The audience sees the actors. The actors see the audience. As the play progresses it is judged. The play changes. The players are changed. The audience is changed. It is a powerful exchange of experience. This doesn't always happen but it can, and directors and writers, perhaps more than anyone else, have the responsibility to see that it does: we have to make the attempt to change perception. The unease that I feel about living in a society that is

115

constructed around male needs and male desires is at its least when I'm working in the theatre—perhaps because it is the art of transformation.

I have a vivid memory of myself at the age of two or three standing at the end of my parents' bed and my father dressing me up in hats, scarves, dresses belonging to my mother. He then led me into the living room and I paraded myself in front of family and friends, my mother included, and was applaud- ed. That was the start of my theatrical career and I hope I have come a long way from that early performance. Someone is always organizing our perceptions and arranging our image and I want to contribute to reorganizing them. I want to understand and acknowledge everything that is female in me but I don't want to be inhibited by ideas of gender. I want to unify and embrace as many realities as I can, to unify and bind many worlds into one whole, but that requires a colossal imagination. I know I have a lot of personal strug- gles ahead of me. I can't imagine what I will be able to imagine five years from now. That is all part of a working process. At this point in time it seems important to articulate some of the splits in the belief that this is one way to go about healing them.

About the contributors

LIANE AUKIN Started acting when she was sixteen. She has written over twenty plays for radio, one of which won a Pye award in 1981, and has had four stage plays produced. She has directed on the Fringe and spent six years with the BBC radio drama department as editor and producer, with over a hundred programmes to her credit. During 1983 and 1984 she was writing for the Crucible Theatre, Sheffield, and directing at the Almeida Theatre, London.

PAM BRIGHTON Has been working as a director since the late 1960s. She was Director of Young People's Work at the Royal Court Theatre, then Artistic Director of the Half Moon Theatre. She moved to Canada, where she directed large-scale classical works during Robin Phillips's regime at Stratford, Ontario. Her productions since her return include *WC PC* at the Half Moon and, among others, *Diary of a Hunger Striker* for Hull Truck Company, of which she became Artistic Director.

CATHERINE HAYES Born and brought up in Liverpool, she is a teacher by training and in 1983 was Head of Modern Languages at a Liverpool comprehensive with twelve years of teaching behind her. She started writing in 1975, and from 1980 to 1981 was Resident Writer at the Liverpool Playhouse. She has written four full-length plays and was voted Most Promising Playwright in the BTA Awards in 1982.

ANN JELLICOE The author of many plays, including *The*

Sport of My Mad Mother which won a prize in the *Observer* Playwriting Competition; *The Knack*, which was later made into a film; *Shelley* and many others, including community plays, translations and plays for children. She worked at the Royal Court, London, where much of her work was first seen and where she later became Literary Manager. In the mid 1970s she and her family moved to Dorset, where she is now Director of the Colway Theatre Trust, which she set up to help produce large-scale community plays based in towns and villages in the West Country.

MARI JENKINS   First trained as an actor but soon decided that her real interest lay backstage. In 1975 she worked as a member of a collective running a theatre created out of a disused warehouse in Rotherhithe and then freelanced at the Oval Arts Centre, where she concentrated on lighting design before joining Monstrous Regiment in 1977 as company stage manager. She recently spent two years at the Cockpit Theatre as technical stage manager, where she also ran workshops for young people, and in 1983 she rejoined Monstrous Regiment.

BRYONY LAVERY   A writer and director, she also ran her own company, Les Oeufs Malades, for which she wrote *Bag, Family Album, Helen and her Friends* and *The Catering Service*. The company became Extraordinary Productions, which was responsible for *Female Trouble*. She has worked for the National Theatre of Brent and has written material for the television series *Revolting Women* as well as for Pamela Stephenson.

DI SEYMOUR   Trained as a graphic designer, she has worked for twelve years designing both sets and costumes for theatre and opera. Her work in both London and the provinces has included seven shows for the RSC; in 1983 she designed the costumes for its production of *Maydays* by David Edgar at the Barbican.

MAGGIE STEED Started acting with the Belgrade, Coventry Theatre in Education Company; was then with Humberside Theatre and Belt and Braces Company. She acted in a season at the Half Moon Theatre which included *Guys and Dolls, Hamlet* and *Arturo Ui*. She played the lead in *Can't Pay Won't Pay* in the West End and was in *Cloud Nine* at the Royal Court. Her television work includes *The Fox, The History Man* and Rita in *Harvey Moon,* of which she will soon be doing a new series. In 1983 she appeared at the National Theatre in Peter Gill's *Small Change*.

SUSAN TODD Has worked as a director since 1968. She directed in rep. for some years, then for the first Women's Season at the Almost Free Theatre and at other Fringe theatres. She joined the Monstrous Regiment Company, both working as director and co-writing plays for the company with Ann Mitchell and David Edgar. She has free-lanced since leaving Monstrous Regiment in 1979, working as Artistic Director for the National Theatre of Brent, directing productions in rep. and teaching.

HARRIET WALTER Started her career doing everything from pub shows to Shakespeare with Common Stock, 7:84 Company, and Paine's Plough. She played in *The Ragged Trousered Philanthropists* for the Joint Stock Campany, then went with Bill Gaskill to the National Theatre. She worked at the Royal Court in *Three More Sleepless Nights, Hamlet* and *The Seagull*. She played in *Nicholas Nickleby,* then did an RSC season, during which her parts included Helena in *All's Well That Ends Well,* Helena in *Midsummer Night's Dream* and Lady Percy in *Henry IV*. She took the lead in the television production of Ian McEwan's *The Imitation Game*.

1

WAWEL HILL AND THE VISTULA EMBANKMENT

THE LEGEND OF THE WAWEL DRAGON

he site where Kraków was built appears to have been chosen by one of the Slavonic tribes at some point between 600 and 800 A.D. The choice was no accident, because for centuries people had been searching for good sites for their permanent settlement – places that were comfortable to live in and easy to defend. They found the ideal site on a broad plateau with the River Vistula flowing through it. There in its flood plain rose a high, limestone hill, which was later named Wawel Hill. A defensive castle was soon built on this hill, and at its foot a small town arose. Its king bore the name Krak, and it is from him that the modern name of Kraków is derived.

Nowadays Wawel Hill does not seem very high to us, but centuries ago Krak's castle would have towered over the district. The cliffs it was built on were very high, full of rifts and deep, hidden caves. One of these caves was the lair of an enormous dragon. The dragon had either been slumbering or living on stored food until people started setting up convenient dwellings near its lair. Or else maybe it only arrived in the area when herds of livestock animals started grazing there. In any case, one day at dawn it appeared by the River Vistula, and from then on it devoured some cattle and sheep on a daily basis. According to rumour, it even carried off young women, and was particularly fond of virgins. The townspeople became afraid to leave their houses. Soon the whole town was in a constant state of terror, and some of the settlers started preparing to leave the place.

King Krak realised that unless he succeeded in defeating the dragon he would have to abandon the newly founded town and lose the lands he had managed to settle. So he summoned his bravest knights and warriors, and offered them his daughter's hand in marriage, along with his entire kingdom as a reward for slaying the dragon.

The chronicles do not record how many of them took on the fight against the dragon, but in any case none of them was successful in vanquishing it. The townspeople lived in greater and greater fear as they helplessly watched the dragon devour more and more animals and carry off the last few virgins. One day a young cobbler's apprentice who was learning to make shoes for the burghers of Kraków came to see King Krak. By all accounts his name was Skuba. He told the king he was very keen to marry the princess, so he would slay the dragon, but to do it he needed a large amount of sulphur, plenty of sheep skins and some mutton fat. King Krak gave orders for Skuba to be provided with everything he asked for. Then the cobbler shut himself up in his cottage, where he spent the whole night busily sewing together the skins, filling them with sulphur and smearing the fleece with fat. Just before dawn he summoned the royal guard to help him carry the enormous ram he had made to the riverbank. At daybreak the dragon woke up as usual, emerged from its cave and happily swallowed the meal prepared for it. But to its surprise, instead of feeling well fed it felt as if a bonfire were burning in its belly, where the flames were growing fiercer by the second – the sulphur was blazing in its bowels. In an effort to put out the flames, the dragon leaped into the Vistula and began to drink greedily. But as the flames refused to die down, it went on and on drinking the river water, while its belly swelled and swelled until it was much too full and burst.

King Krak was overjoyed to hear that the dragon had been slain, and Skuba the cobbler was hailed as a hero by the townspeople who were happy to have regained their peaceful life. The princess was thrilled too, because she considered it a good thing to have a wise and canny husband.

To this day in Kraków people who are admired for dealing with tricky situations in a shrewd way are sometimes described in the local slang as "skubany" – deriving their resourcefulness from Skuba the cobbler.

To this day there is still something left of the dragon – a vast, empty cave, known as "Smocza Jama", or The Dragon's Den. You can go inside it during your visit to the Wawel. As they walk along the Vistula embankment, the children of Kraków stop to admire the dragon's statue which belches fire every now and then, terrifying the youngest ones.

Nowadays the Wawel dragon is Kraków's most famous, best loved mascot. Almost all the tourists take one home with them.

Once you have seen the Dragon's Den you can tour the rest of the Wawel – it is the treasure house of Polish culture and the pride of our nation.

2

THE
MARKETPLACE

THE LEGEND OF THE TWO TOWERS OF ST MARY'S CHURCH

t Mary's Church is the most splendid building in Kraków's Marketplace. It was built circa 1220, originally in Romanesque style, but has been rebuilt many times since then to reach its present shape. It is like a chronicle of Kraków's history, housing many fabulous works of art. No one can fail to be entranced by the altar, which is the work of Veit Stoss, the Master of Nuremberg, who carved it in 1477-1489.

There is a tragic legend connected with the construction of St Mary's church, a tale carrying a warning that is still relevant today.

As we come out onto the Marketplace and catch our first glimpse of the church, our attention is drawn to the two massive towers, one topped with a spire and the other with a cupola, each bearing turrets. In the guidebooks the taller tower is called the Watchtower, and it is from here that the famous St Mary's trumpet-call (known as the "hejnał") rings out every hour. The smaller tower is called the Belltower, because a large bell hangs inside it, which according to legend was carried to the top in the fifteenth century by a single, extremely strong man called Stanisław Ciołek.

So why aren't the towers of St Mary's Church equal in height?

It all happened centuries ago. When the Kraków city authorities made a resolution to rebuild the church, they decided to have two towers guarding its entrance. Two brothers who were famous Kraków builders were given the task of building them. Both were masters of their craft, but as the older brother had been the first to learn the art of building, he had initiated the younger in the secrets of the profession.

On receiving such a large commission they were determined to carry it out to the best of their abilities, but each brother secretly dreamed that his tower would arouse the greater admiration – and so they set about building according to different strategies. The older brother was in a hurry and urged on his workmen. He was relying on having his tower finished first, to prove his mastery of his craft and his superior skills.

Meanwhile, the younger brother was aiming for a slender, tapering construction, and spent a long time preparing the foundations for it. When the older brother had finished his tower, he proudly presented it to the city councillors. But from day to day he was seized by more and more gloomy thoughts, because his younger brother's tower was gradually growing. Envious people began to taunt him, saying he had been such a good teacher that his younger brother had surpassed him in expertise. One evening a quarrel arose between the brothers. Enraged, the older one angrily stuck his knife into the younger man's heart. To conceal the crime, he threw the body into the nearby River Vistula.

After the murder, construction of the northern tower came to a halt, and the city councillors decided not to go on with it. Soon after, both towers were capped, one with a spire and the other with a cupola, and a date was set for the consecration of the church. But the older brother could not live with his conscience so heavily burdened by crime.

On the day when the Bishop performed the consecration of the rebuilt church he confessed his sin to God and to the people gathered in the church. Afterwards, according to one version he threw himself from the tower built by his brother, and according to another he struck himself a fatal blow with the very knife he had used to kill him.

As a warning, the knife still hangs in the Cloth Hall opposite the church, in a place almost every visitor to the Marketplace passes by. You can see it in the passage, chained beneath the vault to remind the citizens and tourists how much evil can be caused by conceit and envy.

Visitors to Kraków should be sure to see St Mary's Church and the Cloth Hall.

3

THE
MARKETPLACE
AND ST MARY'S
SQUARE

THE LEGEND
OF THE TRUMPET CALL
FROM ST MARY'S
TOWER

CRACOVIA

his story concerns the taller tower described in the previous legend, and is famous in many countries, even including Kazakhstan.

The tower is 81 metres in height, and soon after its completion it was named the Watchtower. In those days it was the tallest building in Kraków. Times were not peaceful, and European cities were constantly being attacked by hordes of nomadic Mongol barbarians, or sometimes simply by rapacious neighbouring states, so the Kraków city councillors decided that a sentry should stand on guard in the tower all round the clock, to warn the citizens of approaching danger. For many years a succession of sentries did warn them on several occasions, thanks to which they were able to prepare a timely and effective defence. Serving as the sentry on the Watchtower was an honour attained only by an exceptionally responsible select few men, who were known to all the citizens.

At that time Kraków was not just a beautiful city, but also a rich one, so it could not avoid being raided by the Tatars. The individual Tatar hordes that had been attacking small towns and villages to carry off all sorts of booty, especially captives to sell into slavery, were more and more often joining together to conquer new terrain. The times were dangerous because the heirs to Genghis Khan had extended their realm, occupying Ruthenia and Hungary, and were now starting to extend it into the Polish lands and even further west. This was when the Battle of Legnica was fought, one of several battles that determined the future of all Europe, at which the Polish Duke Henryk the Pious halted the Tatar advance, but suffered great losses in the process. He paid the highest price, killed on the field of battle along with most of his knights, but the Mongol expansion was stopped, and soon ceased to be a direct threat to Europe.

One day in 1240, at early dawn when the city was still asleep, the Tatar cavalry appeared not far from the fortified walls. The only person to notice the danger was the sentry on the St Mary's Church Watchtower. Immediately he began to sound the alarm call, rousing the troops and the citizens from their beds. And he played his trumpet without stopping in all directions, to warn as many people as possible.

When the Tatars stormed the city, their first target was the sentry who had thwarted their attempt to catch the defenders off guard. A Tatar arrow pierced his throat and cut him off in mid-note of the alarm call he was playing. But it was too late for them to capture and pillage Kraków. The soldiers and citizens had appeared on the walls and turrets by now, and fought off the Tatar attack. The sentry who had saved the city at the cost of his own life was buried with great honours, and the memory of his sacrifice is still alive today, commemorated by the trumpet-call that resounds from St Mary's Tower. Played to all four quarters of the globe, it marks each hour, and is cut short on the same note as it was by the Tatar arrow almost 800 years ago. First the trumpeter plays in the direction of Wawel Hill, in honour of the king, then he turns towards the Town Hall Tower out of respect for the councillors, then towards the Florian Gate to greet arriving guests, and finally towards the Little Marketplace to play for the merchants and citizens.

Over the years the Kraków trumpet-call – known as the "hejnał" – has become a symbol of self-sacrifice for your country. Programme One on Polish Radio broadcasts it nationwide every day at twelve noon at the start of its main news programme, and many other Polish-language radio stations all round the world broadcast it too, to confirm their ties to their home country.

The "hejnał" is so strongly associated with Kraków that ceremonial sessions of the City Council are opened by the sentry from St Mary's Tower, who is invited to other Kraków ceremonies and events too, including football matches played by the local club, Cracovia, which was founded in 1906.

According to many travellers, the legend of the St Mary's trumpet-call is told on several continents. You can even hear it on the steppes of Kazakhstan and Mongolia, where the story of the bugler who thwarted the capture of Kraków is known as the Legend of the Golden Trumpet.

A tour of Kraków should include a visit to the Town Hall Tower in the Marketplace, which used to be the headquarters of the city authorities.

4

THE SUBURB
OF ZWIERZYNIEC
AND THE
MARKETPLACE

THE LEGEND
OF LAJKONIK
THE HOBBYHORSE

here is another Kraków legend connected with the Tatars, who were constantly invading Polish territory for a large part of the thirteenth century.

Protected by strong fortifications, centuries ago Kraków was a large, buzzing city. As usual in the area surrounding a city, numerous villages and settlements arose beyond its walls. Their inhabitants were renowned for various arts and crafts, and often worked to order for Kraków's merchants, burghers and knights. One of these settlements, situated on the left bank of the River Vistula, was called Zwierzyniec. It was the home of the raftsmen who floated goods along the river, mainly heavy tree trunks. It was not easy to be a raftsman. The work demanded great strength, fortitude and endurance. Not surprisingly, the raftsmen retained some of the old Slavonic wildness in them and were not regarded as fearful or submissive people.

According to the legend, one day one of the Tatar hordes tried to capture the city in the daytime, taking advantage of its open gates. To get close to the city walls quickly they chose a track along the river leading to the Vistula Gate. This track ran through the raftsmen's village, Zwierzyniec. To the invaders' surprise, the raftsmen did not run away, but stood in the path of the Tatar cavalry. This unexpected defence was extremely successful – the raftsmen not only drove the Tatars away from the city,

but
also
killed
the Tatar
khan him-
self. Proud of
their victory, they
dressed one of their
number in the khan's clothes and seated him on a cap-
tured horse. Surrounded by his comrades, he set off for
Kraków, where the grateful citizens rewarded the raftsmen with gold and a feast. This was the first procession
led by the "khan" on his horse, and with time it came to
be called the Lajkonik Pageant.

Nowadays, every year in June, during Corpus Christi week, Lajkonik and his grand retinue make their way along the same route as centuries ago, from Zwierzyniec, which is now a suburb of Kraków, along the River Vistula to the former Vistula Gate. Lajkonik, as the raftsman character is called, "sits" on a wooden hobbyhorse, dressed in the rich apparel of the Tatar khan. He is played by one of the residents of Zwierzyniec.

A large number of tourists and Cracovians wait for him to come by, to see this colourful and curious spectacle – the procession consisting of Lajkonik, his standard-bearers and choir numbers about thirty people. According to tradition, if Lajkonik touches you with his decorated wooden mace you will have good luck for the whole year to come – single girls can count on finding a fiancé, the poor can count on some money, and everyone can be sure of good repute. That must be why Lajkonik tries his best not to leave anyone out, and the game goes on for several hours in the Marketplace. Just as once upon a time the grateful citizens rewarded the raftsmen, so nowadays the Mayor and his councillors receive Lajkonik and his entourage at a feast beneath the Town Hall Tower and hand them a symbolic reward. Many tourists arrange their trip to Poland in time to see the spectacle and be touched by the Tatar-Kraków mace for good luck.

On a visit to the Castle on Wawel Hill you can see many exhibits connected with the Turkish invasions. You can also visit the Norbertine Church in Zwierzyniec, which is the starting point for the Lajkonik Pageant.

5

THE
MARKETPLACE

THE LEGEND OF THE PIGEONS OF KRAKÓW MARKETPLACE

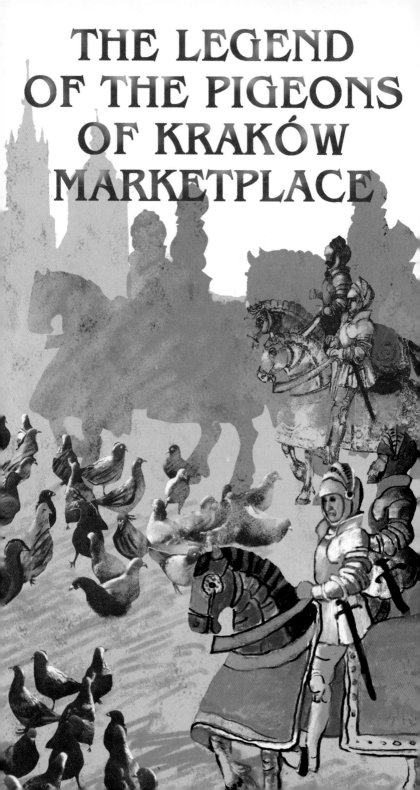

rakòw's Marketplace, which is one of the finest city-centre squares in Europe, was established in the second half of the thirteenth century, not long after the city's foundation in 1257, and soon became the site of several events that have been memorialized in legend.

The Marketplace is the heart of Kraków, the focal point of life in the city as the citizens regularly pass through it, often at least a dozen times a day, in the course of their ordinary business, and it is where they come to rest and drink in the atmosphere of a thousand years of history. It is also the place they miss most of all when they are away, and that they always come back to. The Marketplace is the site of St Mary's Church and the Cloth Hall, which are already familiar to us from two earlier legends, and it is also the destination for the Lajkonik Pageant, as described in a third. No one can visit Kraków without spending a few hours in the Marketplace, taking a break at one of the many charming cafes and restaurants. As you admire the largest square in Europe, you cannot fail to notice the thousands of pigeons that are always there in the same spot, on the St Jan's Street and Floriańska Street side. Even though they cause the citizens a lot of bother to do with keeping the place clean, no one ever tries to drive them away. Just about every child in Kraków has been here to feed them at least once in their lives, and lots of people go on feeding them into their old age.

So why are the Cracovians so kind to their pigeons?

At the end of the thirteenth century Duke Henryk IV Probus came to the throne in Kraków. He did not bear the title of king, because Poland was still divided into a number of dukedoms and did not yet have a single ruler.

27

Duke Henryk wanted to unite the Polish lands and become their king. As in those days it was the Pope who crowned rulers as kings and anointed them in the name of God, the duke had to seek the consent of Pope Nicholas IV, who had come to the Papal throne during the closing era of the Crusades, when Acre, the final Crusader stronghold, was lost to the Saracens.

Henryk began preparations for the journey to Rome. However, he did not have enough money for it – he had used it all up equipping his numerous company of knights, thanks to whom he had already managed to join together several of the formerly disunited Polish territories. According to the legend, in his search for a way to solve his problems he consulted a sorceress. She promised to help, but imposed a condition. She told the duke that she would change his company of knights into pigeons, who would spend an entire day carrying pebbles to the Kraków Marketplace. During the night the pebbles would turn into gold, but the knights would only change back into people if the duke returned to Kraków with the royal crown. After conferring with his knights, Henryk IV agreed to the sorceress' condition. And so the splendid company of knights was soon changed into a flock of pigeons. The pigeons busily carried in the pebbles, and by evening there was a large pile of them towering in the Marketplace, which changed into gold overnight. The duke loaded the gold into coffers and travelling bags, and set off with his retinue for Rome. The pigeons stayed where they were, waiting for his return.

Nowadays we can be certain that the duke never reached Rome. Apparently he got as far as Venice, where he stopped for a long time. Some say that several of the enchanted knights flew after him, which is said to be the origin of the Venetian pigeons in St Mark's Square. Henryk's enemies – including many other dukes who were eager to take the throne – told his successors that he spent all the money on entertainments and pleasure. But we have other historical sources too, which claim that Henryk IV was involved in numerous armed skirmishes, where he could have lost the gold. Times were truly dangerous: in Germany Rudolf of Habsburg had just come to power, the forefather of a great European dynasty, William Tell was at war in Switzerland, and the Hanseatic League was in the process of being established.

In about 1289 Henryk returned to the Wawel without the crown, and to the day he died he never had the courage to stand in the Marketplace and behold his faithful company of knights. He died the next year, apparently poisoned. The knights never regained their human form, and for over 700 years now they have been fluttering about as pigeons, keeping a watchful eye on the passers-by, looking out for their duke and waiting for the spell to be broken.

Their sacrifice may not have been in vain, for some thirty years later, in 1320, the next duke of Kraków, Władysław Łokietek, did gain the crown from Pope John XXII and became the new king of Poland. His son, Kazimierz, known as the Great, restored splendour and power to the entire kingdom. Kraków began to develop very rapidly and was soon one of the most important cities in Europe, thanks in part to the university founded by Kazimierz in 1364, which is now called the Jagiellonian University. There a famous congress of the monarchs of Europe was held, to which Kazimierz invited the German emperor, Charles IV, and the rulers of many other states.

The Cracovians haven't forgotten their noble knights and will look after them as long as the Marketplace exists, waiting with them for the spell to be broken. Maybe the bewitching magic of the place is in the pigeons themselves.

During your visit to Kraków, be sure to see the Collegium Maius, the oldest building at the University, and the museum it houses.

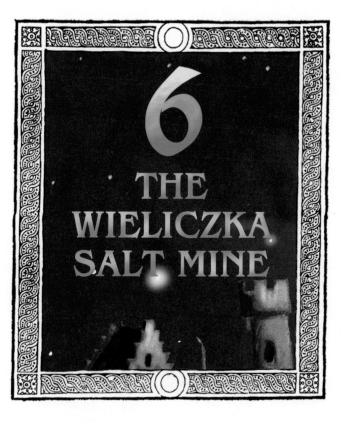

6
THE
WIELICZKA
SALT MINE

THE LEGEND OF ST KINGA'S RING

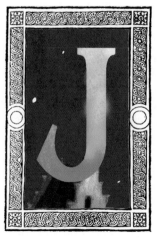

J ust under thirty minutes drive from the centre of Kraków there is a town called Wieliczka. Nowadays it is really a suburb of Kraków. But when Princess Kinga came to Poland in 1239, it was a long way from the Wawel to Wieliczka. Wieliczka is the site of the famous Salt Mine, which is listed among UNESCO's top World Cultural Heritage monuments, and is the oldest working mine in the world, active without a break since the thirteenth century to the present day.

The following legend is about Kraków, Kinga, Wieliczka and the salt mine, and testifies to the great wisdom of Poland's queen in those days.

Duke Bolesław, known to his contemporaries as the Shy, who was then ruling from the Wawel, was in search of a wife far from the country. As is often the case with rulers, his plan to marry was the result of a political strategy and was designed to strengthen the power of his dynasty. Duke Bolesław, who belonged to the Piast family that had ruled Poland since it first became an independent state, was planning to contract a marriage with the daughter of the King of Hungary, who belonged to the Arpad family. Her name was Kinga, and she was the beloved daughter of Bela IV and Maria Laskazis, daughter of the Byzantine emperor.

The beautiful Hungarian princess consented to the marriage, but as she was a long way ahead of her age in terms of intellect, she asked her father for an unusual dowry. She didn't want any gold, silver or precious fabrics – instead she asked for something that would allow her to increase the prosperity of her new home country. As in those days salt mines were the equivalent of today's oil wells, the Hungarian King Bela gave his daughter one of the salt mines that were making the Hungarians richer. But the mine was far away from Poland, so the princess realised that it would be very difficult to take advantage of the present. As she watched the miners working in the pits, she wished she could take the mine to her new country with her. So she took off a valuable ring and threw it into the deepest shaft, while praying to St Francis of Assisi and St Clare for their help.

Soon after, amid a company of Polish and Hungarian knights, Kinga set off on her way to Poland. During her first few months at the Castle in Kraków, she came to know her new subjects. The longer she was among them, the more she dreamed of contributing to their welfare. One day she suggested to Duke Bolesław that they should go and look for a place where they could found a mine and extract salt. Next day, a large retinue including the duke and his wife left the Wawel, and towards evening they stopped at a small forestry village called Wieliczka. Without knowing why, through pure intuition Kinga felt sure they need seek no further – this was the place where they should dig. Next morning the local people and the duke's servants carried out the first mining work. We do not know if the first blocks of salt were found that day or a few days later, but we do know that Kinga was present when they were extracted. She even went into the newly mined pit and joyfully fetched out block after block of salt, displaying them to the assembled company. Suddenly, among the grey and white rocks, she saw something glittering like gold. She bent down again and picked up a ring – the very one she had thrown into the shaft her father had given her in Hungary. Now she was certain this was the right place to build the mine.

The mine brought great wealth to Kraków and Poland, improved the people's standard of living and made them more prosperous. To this day it is a real treasure, visited by millions of tourists. Kinga never stopped looking for ways to help her country develop, took great care of its citizens and did many more good things for them. It is said that her dowry paid for the rebuilding of Kraków after a Tatar raid, and it was her financial resources that helped the city to be formally founded according to Magdeburg law in 1257. After the death of her husband she assumed the habit of a nun and went to live in the convent of the Order of St Clare in Nowy Sącz that she herself had founded, and that is where she lies at eternal rest. Some years after her death she was canonized as St Kinga, one of the patron saints of Poland.

It is well worth taking the time to visit the Wieliczka Salt Mine, to see how miners did their job several hundred years ago.

7

THE
WAWEL
CATHEDRAL

THE LEGEND OF THE "HEART" OF THE BELL

he biggest bell in Poland, which is also one of the biggest in the world, hangs in the tower of the royal cathedral on Wawel Hill. It weighs almost eleven tons, has a diameter of about 2.5 metres and is about 2 metres high. It was endowed for the glory of God and Poland in 1520 by King Zygmunt I the Old, and is associated with him for all time through its name – Zygmunt's Bell.

During the reign of Zygmunt I the Polish kingdom was a military and economic power, with strong ties to other ruling families in Europe – for example, Zygmunt's wife was Queen Bona, of the Italian Sforza dynasty.

Zygmunt's Bell is regarded as one of the prime symbols of Polish patriotism, and is only rung to mark exceptionally significant events, or during church festivals and ceremonies. Therefore the clapper – which in Polish is called the "heart" of the bell – is rarely used, but over the years it has become associated with the following legend.

The story tells how one day the daughter of one the eight people needed to set the bell in motion just happened to be in the bell tower. That day, the bell was ringing to mark some great event. The girl had come to give her father an urgent message, but she had to wait until the bell-ringers had finished their work. This girl was unhappily in love, and couldn't think about anything except her emotions. As she waited she became lost in thought, dreaming that the man she loved would ask for her hand. When her father asked her why she had come, the question shook her abruptly from her dreams, and instead of telling him the real reason why she had come to the bell tower she recklessly told him about the man she loved, and that he took no notice of her. Meanwhile Zygmunt's Bell was still ringing. Her father smiled and said:

If your heart is unhappy, look to the heart of the bell.
It is beating for all of us, for our glory and welfare.
Your heart must be just as strong and mighty, and
then maybe your dreams will come true.

He was only trying to encourage his daughter and cheer her up, but she took his words seriously. As soon as the bell stopped ringing, she pressed her face against the clapper, which was still warm from striking, and she asked God to make the "heart" of the bell give her heart strength and to arouse her beloved's interest in her. Days passed, maybe weeks or months, but still she went on waiting for her dreams to come true. Finally the man she had chosen did notice that she was different from the other girls of her age. We don't know exactly how it came about, but she did become his wife. And as she didn't keep her secret hidden, soon more and more young women were trying to touch the warm bell clapper and voice their dreams.

Nowadays, if you visit the Wawel Cathedral you can go up the bell tower, and even though it's a tiring climb, many tourists make the effort every day, including lots of people who want to touch the bell clapper. In fact it is cold and still, but sometimes it helps people who are in love, or looking for love. It has even become customary to touch it with your left hand, the one that is closer to your heart. So it is not at all unusual to see both women and men stopping for a moment to touch it – almost everyone does, maybe voicing their dreams as they do so, and perhaps some of them even come true. After all, true faith and strong hearts can perform miracles.

While touring the Wawel Cathedral and the bell tower don't miss the tombs of the Polish kings. The Church on the Rock is also worth visiting

8

KAZIMIERZ

THE LEGEND OF THE JEWISH WEDDING

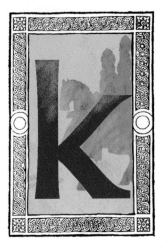

azimierz, which in olden days was a separate town, is now one of the best known districts of Kraków. It is named after Kazimierz III the Great, who founded it in 1335 not far from the dynamically developing city of Kraków.

Because of its proximity to Kraków, in the fifteenth century Kazimierz was gradually settled by large numbers of Jews who had been expelled from other European kingdoms and dukedoms, and who came here to do business. In time, more and more synagogues were built alongside the city's many churches and convents. The Jewish community developed rapidly, and soon in the area now centred on Szeroka, Józef and Jakub Streets an almost independent Jewish Town had come into being.

Nowadays Kazimierz is a must for any tourist, containing many cultural sites that testify to the co-existence of the Poles and the Jews. Tourists searching for signs of Jewish culture can visit the synagogues in Kazimierz, especially the Tempel, the Isaac and the Popper. The Remuh synagogue and the neighbouring cemetery also attract large crowds of tourists from all over the world, and it is with this particular place that the legend of the Jewish wedding is connected. For centuries this legend has acted as a warning to those of the Jewish faith.

One day in the Jewish Town an ostentatious wedding was held opposite the Remuh synagogue. The bride and groom were happy to be starting their life together, but their parents were even happier. Through this marriage they were uniting two of the richest Jewish families, and had great hopes for a prosperous future. The wedding was magnificent and sumptuous. The hosts and guests were so completely absorbed in singing, eating and drinking that they stopped paying attention to the passage of time. They went on celebrating for far longer than they had planned, continuing their revels into the early hours of the Sabbath – a holy day for all Jews. They ignored the rabbi's appeals and warnings as he anxiously noted the turn the wedding was taking, and tried to prevent them from committing sacrilege. Time went by, it was already evening on the Sabbath and the sun had long since set, but still the revellers went on enjoying themselves. Suddenly a very strong wind began to blow, and the ground and neighbouring houses started shaking. The band fell silent, the dancing stopped, and the dining tables overturned. The bride and groom, their parents and all the other revellers looked around them in terror, seeking the help of the rabbi, but it was already too late. The earthquake shook the entire Jewish Town, but only in one place did the earth cave in – right under the feet of the banqueters. They all fell beneath it, and the ground went on shaking and moving until it had covered them over, making a natural grave. None of the Jews who witnessed the tragedy had the courage to try and dig out the buried revellers. Several days later they were still so terrified that they decided to build a low wall right round the grave – once the site of the wedding party – so that no one should ever commit any such act again.

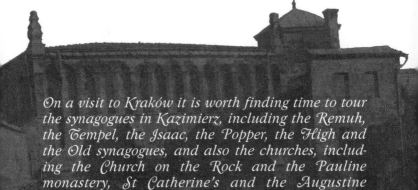

For centuries nothing has changed in front of the synagogue. The entire walled area, located on what is now Szeroka Street, has remained vacant for hundreds of years, as a warning not to break the Law. And they say that since then no Jewish wedding has ever been celebrated in Kazimierz on a Friday. Those who visit the site today can see that opposite the entrance to the Remuh synagogue there is still a fenced, undeveloped flower-bed – a dreadful reminder for those of the Jewish faith.

On a visit to Kraków it is worth finding time to tour the synagogues in Kazimierz, including the Remuh, the Tempel, the Isaac, the Popper, the High and the Old synagogues, and also the churches, including the Church on the Rock and the Pauline monastery, St Catherine's and the Augustine monastery, and Corpus Christi and the monastery of the Lateran Canons

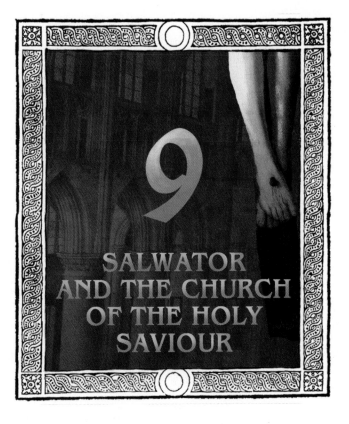

9

SALWATOR
AND THE CHURCH
OF THE HOLY
SAVIOUR

THE LEGEND
OF THE POOR FIDDLER
AND GOD'S MERCY

alwator means "The Saviour". Centuries ago this hill was part of the village of Zwierzyniec on the outskirts of Kraków, and is regarded as one of the finest places in the city. This enchanting spot is an absolute must for anyone making plans for sightseeing in Kraków, not just because of the nearby Kościuszko Mound or the almost 900-year-old Church of the Holy Saviour.

The church is said to have been built by the Polish magnate Piotr Włast, the legendary founder of seventy-seven churches. The Bishop of Kraków prophesied to him that he would regain his sight on condition that he founded seven churches and three monasteries. But the magnate was so conceited that he built as many as seventy churches and thirty monasteries. However, he did not regain his sight. Once he finally realised that he had committed a sin, he started all over again, building three monasteries and seven churches. One of them was the Church of the Holy Saviour, dating from circa 1148. We should add that according to legend, happily the magnate did regain his sight.

This church houses an old icon entitled The Crucifixion of Christ, which is an unusual representation of Jesus dressed in a long, lovely robe and a rich pair of shoes. There is a fiddler kneeling at his feet, and one of the valuable shoes is slipping into his hands. This picture presents what may have been the first Polish testimony to God's mercy, and this is the legend featured in the picture.

51

First led by the legendary Krak, the Slavs who had settled by the River Vistula soon built up a powerful state. From the ninth century onwards, when the mission of Sts Cyril and Methodius took place, Christianity had begun to spread to these lands. The first Polish duke to accept the Christian faith, which happened in 996 A.D., was called Mieszko. To commemorate the event he was given a magnificent crucifix. But as he was only just starting to understand the Christian faith, he did not want Jesus hanging on the cross to be naked like a beggar. So he gave orders for rich robes to be made for the Saviour, and also a pair of shoes adorned with gold and pearls. Soon the crucifix became the site of a cult and was visited by many pilgrims who believed in its unusual power to perform miracles.

One day a very poor fiddler came to appeal to Jesus for help. He was bringing up a son alone, and as he couldn't leave the child without care he had no way of earning a living. They were extremely impoverished, but they managed to live happily, as long as the child did not fall ill, because the fiddler had no money for medical treatment. So he came up to the Cross, knelt down, and while playing a moving tune on his fiddle, he told Jesus all about his adversity. And then a miracle occurred – one of the valuable shoes fell from Christ's foot and landed in front of the fiddler. He thanked God, took the shoe and went out into the marketplace to exchange it for some money. But as soon as he showed the merchants what he had to sell, they immediately called the city guards, who arrested him for theft. Neither the merchants nor the guards would believe it was the Lord Jesus Himself who had given him the shoe to save his only son. Nor did the city authorities believe him, and that very day they condemned him to death. The fiddler had no idea how to persuade them of the truth. The execution was due to take place early the next morning. The fiddler's last wish, which is the condemned man's traditional right, filled everyone with amazement. In despair he asked to play his fiddle for the Lord Jesus on the cross once more before his death.

Early next morning, before a large number of curious onlookers, the fiddler knelt before the Cross again, and wept as he played his tune. All those present became aware of the father's desperation. Before their very eyes, once again the Lord Jesus dropped His precious shoe into the musician's hands. Yet again the Saviour had heard his plea and answered it. Naturally the fiddler was released, and some time later a painter immortalised the miracle of God's mercy on the icon that still hangs in the church today.

Unfortunately, the crucifix is no longer in Kraków. At a time of troubles it was removed to Numena, a small town near Ancona in Italy, but the memory of the event has survived in the story passed down the generations by the citizens of Kraków, and of course the icon showing Jesus giving his shoe to the fiddler is still part of the altar screen in the Church of the Holy Saviour.

Perhaps in a small way this legendary event is linked with the fact that it was in Kraków, just before the Second World War, that Sister Faustina saw visions of Divine Mercy, and it was in Kraków, at Łagiewniki, that the Sanctuary of the Divine Mercy was built. Every year it receives hundreds of thousands of visitors from all over the world, who come to make ardent requests, because they believe they can count on the help of Our Saviour, who extends His mercy to everyone.

Visitors to Kraków should be sure to see the Sanctuary of the Divine Mercy at Łagiewniki, a site for Christian pilgrims from all over the world.

10

THE
WAWEL
CASTLE

THE LEGEND
OF THE KRAKÓW
"CHAKRAM",
THE SACRED STONE
OF THE HINDUS

n Sanskrit the word "cha-kram" means literally a ring or a circle. According to Hindu mythology and con-temporary Hindu initiates, centuries ago the god Shiva cast onto the Earth seven stones concentrating cosmic and earth-ly energy. According to Hindu belief, these round stones, called "chakrams", are meant to renew life-giving forces and guarantee protection against evil. They create a circle that protects the world. They say that one of the chakrams was cast onto the Wawel Hill and is located beneath the Royal Castle. The others fell in Delhi, Jerusalem, Mecca, Delphi, Rome and Velehrad. Thus Kraków is one of the world's most sacred sites for Hindus. Just as Christians go to the Holy Land and Muslims go to Mecca, so Hindus make pilgrim-ages to their holy cities, including Kraków.

There is no room here for the story of Shiva and the other gods of Hindu mythology, so we will not go back thousands of years to explain why Shiva protected the Earth with chakrams. We shall only go back to the period between the First and Second World Wars, and the visit to Kraków of a group of Hindus who asked to be given access to the cellar in the west wing of the Royal Castle. There they gathered in St Gereon's crypt, where they spent a long time standing still in meditation. Apparently at the time people noticed a mysterious radiance emanating from the direction of the crypt. And that was enough for the most recent of Kraków's legends to arise in the twentieth century – the legend of the energy-producing effect of the chakram located under the west wing of the Castle.

If it does exist, the chakram is said to emit energy through the power of man's inner strength, the power of auto-suggestion which can mobilise enormous potential in the human body. Perhaps it has already helped someone – it certainly hasn't done any harm. However, for several years now the site where it is supposed to be located is no longer accessible to visitors. Yet as in Kraków to be truly legendary a story must have been told for more than a hundred years, perhaps in time visitors to Wawel Hill will not only be able to see the dragon's cave, but also to stand at the site where the chakram releases its energy.